Dear Reader,

Most of the people I work with in my office know two things about me: I'm horrible with clichés and I have a tendency—a little, tiny, teeny-weeny tendency—to be dramatic. In fact, it has been said on more than one occasion that no one could be more dramatic than I am.

So naturally I set out to prove them all wrong.

My heroine, Corinne Weatherby, is definitely the most dramatic person I know. This is why it takes the calming influence of a man like my hero, Matthew Relic, to settle her down. But as Corinne quickly discovers, when it comes to love and passion and dancing, there's nothing calm about Matthew! He's absolutely one of my favorite heroes. You just can't help but fall in love with him. Neither can Corinne.

This book is for everyone who has gone in search of *true* love, only to find it smack-dab under their noses.

Enjoy!

Stephanie Doyle

P.S. I love to hear from readers. Come visit my Web site at www.stephaniedoyle.net.

Could she really have an affair with Matthew?

Why had Corinne never noticed how good-looking he was? He was gorgeous! But he was her friend...could they have an affair and still be friends?

"Matthew, I don't know about this."

Somberly he nodded. "We *are* taking a big risk."

"It's just that this is all so new, so scary," she added.

"Scary? It's not like you could get sick," he assured her.

Corinne made a face. "I'm not worried about getting sick. I'm worried you'll be disappointed." After all, it had been a while for her. Did one forget how to do these things?

He shrugged his shoulders. "I'm pretty easy to please."

"I'm worried you'll hate me in the morning when you realize..."

"As long as they have chicken on the menu..." he said at the same time.

They stopped speaking. Then Matthew got a pained look on his face. "We're not talking about the same thing, are we?"

Stephanie Doyle

One True Love?

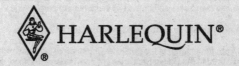

HARLEQUIN®

TORONTO • NEW YORK • LONDON
AMSTERDAM • PARIS • SYDNEY • HAMBURG
STOCKHOLM • ATHENS • TOKYO • MILAN • MADRID
PRAGUE • WARSAW • BUDAPEST • AUCKLAND

To the lunch crowd—especially Carolyn, Jeanine,
Dawn, Mike, Bill, Paul and Chuck, with occasional
special guest appearances from Matt and Jim.
You guys manage to keep me laughing and sane
in a sometimes insane place.

May the bridge always be burning
when we get to it!

ISBN 0-373-44176-2

ONE TRUE LOVE?

Copyright © 2003 by Stephanie Doyle.

Visit us at www.eHarlequin.com

Printed in U.S.A.

ABOUT THE AUTHOR

Stephanie Doyle began her writing career in eighth grade when she was given an assignment to write in a journal every day. Her own life being routine, she used the opportunity to write her own sequel to the *Star Wars* movies. One hundred and six handwritten pages later, she discovered her lifelong dream—to be a writer. Currently, Stephanie resides in South Jersey with her cat, Alexandria Hamilton Doyle. Single, she still waits for Mr. Right to sweep her off her feet. She vows that whoever he is, he'll decorate the cover of at least one of her books.

Books by Stephanie Doyle

HARLEQUIN DUETS
65—DOWN-HOME DIVA
88—BAILY'S IRISH DREAM

SILHOUETTE INTIMATE MOMENTS

792—UNDISCOVERED HERO

Don't miss any of our special offers. Write to us at the following address for information on our newest releases.

Harlequin Reader Service
U.S.: 3010 Walden Ave., P.O. Box 1325, Buffalo, NY 14269
Canadian: P.O. Box 609, Fort Erie, Ont. L2A 5X3

Dear Reader,

Welcome to Harlequin Flipside! If you love a dash of wit and cleverness with your romance, then this is the line for you. These stories are for readers who appreciate that, if love makes the world go around, the ride is a lot more fun with a few laughs along the way.

Leading off the launch, we have *USA TODAY* bestselling author Millie Criswell with *Staying Single*. This heroine is determined to remain single—three almost weddings is enough for one girl, isn't it?—no matter what her marriage-focused mother says. But after meeting a certain photojournalist, she just might have second thoughts....

Rounding out the month is Stephanie Doyle's *One True Love?* Believing that each person has only one true love, our heroine is in a bit of a dilemma. Turns out that the guy she picked isn't the same guy who's captured her thoughts. This calls for some rearranging...fast!

Look for two Harlequin Flipside books every month at your favorite bookstore. And check us out online at www.HarlequinFlipside.com. We hope you enjoy this new line of romantic comedy stories.

See you next month!

Wanda Ottewell
Editor

Mary-Theresa Hussey
Executive Editor

1

"I'M LEAVING YOU," Corinne Weatherby exclaimed.

She slammed the door behind her, leaning against it as if the power of her own words had thrust her against the door. She spotted the second door open on the other side of the office and winced. She'd forgotten about the filing room. She crossed the room and slammed that door, too, for good measure. And in case the man sitting behind the office desk hadn't heard her, she repeated, "I'm leaving you, Brendan. I mean it this time."

Not looking up from his busy task of bouncing one silver ball against another on the same pendulum, Brendan waved off her statement. "You're going on vacation, Corinne. You'll be back in two weeks."

With a toss of her flaming-red curls, Corinne explained the situation to him. "Not two weeks. A lifetime. I'm leaving you symbolically."

This time Brendan did look up at her with his soulful blue eyes. She almost caved until she realized it was confusion she read in those eyes and not anguish over her departure. "Does that mean you're not really going anywhere? Is this some kind of meditation thing?"

She closed her eyes and summoned patience. Maybe her true love wasn't the brightest of men, but he was hers. Or at least he would be after they'd played out the script. She had practically written the whole plot in her head. Every line was committed to memory. Every piece of choreography had been rehearsed a thousand times in her mind. So far everything was on cue...except for the second open door. But there were some things that Corinne simply could not predict.

Pulling a bit on the length of her tiny grasshopper-green skirt—an atypical length for her but the chosen costume for this particular farewell scene—Corinne positioned herself accordingly to show off her shapely, albeit short, legs. Just a taste of what he was going to miss. "What I meant to say is that although I will be back in two weeks, when I return, figuratively, I will be dead to you."

This time Brendan was motivated enough by her words to stand. He sauntered over to where she stood with her back still against the door to the filing room. In the few steps it took to reach her, Corinne could see the transition in his face.

The man was like a chameleon. He adapted his expressions perfectly to the current situation. For this confrontation he brought out the big guns: the cute, cuddly-boy routine.

He sure knew how to play rough. She was a particular sucker for this one. Had he gone with smooth and seductive, she might have stood a better chance.

No. No, she told herself firmly. She had to be strong. Cuddly-boy face or no, this was their future she was fighting for. Corinne shored up her defense system.

But it was so hard. The soft blond hair that was perfectly trimmed, the wide-open blue eyes framed in a face golden from more than a few hours spent at the tanning salon, and the pouting mouth that had made her knees buckle more times than she could count, all added to the package. Today he had chosen a powder-blue shirt, which highlighted his eyes and coordinating dark-blue suspenders. Those suspenders made her want to pull on them until they snapped against his gym-hardened pecs. Not to cause him pain or anything. Just because she thought it might be fun. Yes, this man was her destiny. This man was her one true love.

If only he would wake up and smell the donuts.

"Babe, what do you mean you're going to be dead to me? I'm still going to want to see you when you get back."

Such sincerity. Such caring. Such *bull*. Corinne knew him too well to believe his words. What she needed to do was show him how awful his life would be without her. "Stay with me, Brendan. I said *you're* going to be dead to *me*. Which means the only place you will see me is in the lunchroom."

"But why, babe? We have had a good thing going. And I think we've got some unfinished business," he said slyly.

He was talking about the other night when she had kicked him out of her condo before they made it to the bedroom. Corinne was a modern woman. She was perfectly ready to go to bed with the man she knew to be her destiny. But she wanted it to be perfect. Perfect meant that when she went to bed with Brendan, he would stop going to bed with all the other women. It was sort of her rule. Until he was ready to make that commitment, the door to her bedroom would remain locked.

"Can you honestly tell me you're ready to give up the others?"

"Others?" he asked in that innocently boyish tone he had mastered.

Corinne sighed. "The others, Brendan. The other women."

"If that's what you want…"

For a moment Corinne's hopes were raised, but then a name flashed behind her eyes and she remembered what had started her off on this particular script in the first place. "Ah-hah!" she shouted, as she thrust her index finger into his impossibly firm chest.

"Ah-hah what?"

"You told me the other night that you were going to stop seeing all the other women. You said you wanted to commit to me. Then I had to hear about Marjorie from human resources from Sally in administration. Marjorie from human resources? I mean, really."

Brendan immediately went for the innocent face. Not that he could fool her. Corinne knew each of his faces too intimately. She'd studied them. As a student of theater and acting she had from time to time graded his expressions. It was why they were so perfect for each other. He couldn't fool her. He couldn't charm his way out of messy situations with her. Once he understood that she knew him for who he was but still loved him, she was sure he would come around to her way of thinking.

Or at least almost sure.

Reasonably sure.

Pretty darn sure.

"Honey, Marjorie and I are just friends. So we went out for a couple of drinks. We were with a bunch of other people from the office."

"Like who?" This was his fatal flaw. He could be a smooth liar, but he could never back up a lie once he began it. *Oh, Brendan, is there anyone else on this planet who could love you?* Corinne didn't think so.

"Like…like…uh…uh…Relic was there!"

Corinne actually had to laugh. Although her script did call for a stoic face and a resolute manner throughout the entire breakup scene, this was too funny not to chuckle. "Matthew Relic was at the bar with you and Marjorie from human resources? I don't think so."

"No, really, he was," Brendan continued futilely. "You can ask him."

She shook her head sharply. "Brendan, Matthew and I are friends. If I ask him, he'll tell me the truth."

"Oh." The man deflated before her eyes. But he was quick to rebound. "Sweetheart, babe, you know you're the only one I really *care* about."

It was the emphasis on the word *care* that got her. It always did. "I know you care about me, Brendan, but I want more."

"And I want to give you more," Brendan said with a smile, while he brought his hands up to cover her petite shoulders. "You deserve the best, honey. I know that. What kind of fool do you take me for?"

"I don't think you're a fool, Brendan. But you have to understand I can't go on this way. The other people in this company are laughing at me."

"But you always like to be the center of attention," he volleyed.

"I like to be the center of attention when I put myself there. I don't want anyone else to do that for me. Now for the last time, are you going to stop seeing other women?" Here it comes, she thought, the big finale to scene one.

Brendan shoved his hands deep into his suit pockets, then quickly took them out and smoothed out the wrinkles he had made. He shuffled his feet and looked to the ceiling for what Corinne could only assume was divine intervention. "It's just that you know how I am, babe. I can't help it if other women need me. I mean what about the man shortage? If I give up all the others, I'll be contributing to it rather than helping it. That's just not the kind of guy I am."

He actually thought he was being noble. Corinne couldn't stop the pain in her heart. Not that she hadn't predicted exactly this outcome, but still, it took her a moment to compose herself. The touch of wetness to make her eyes look that much shinier would not be difficult to fake.

"Fine. But know this, Brendan. I'm the only woman you know who has seen the real you and has still managed to fall in love with you. You'll never get from them what you could have gotten from me. Once I come back from this vacation, you'll know what it means to be truly alone."

BRAVO! Bravo!

Matthew Relic cheered silently from his current prison—the filing-room closet attached to Brendan's office. Obviously, Corinne hadn't seen him in here when she slammed the door, and Golden Boy must have forgotten that he had come in to get one of the client folders a few minutes prior to Corinne's grand entrance. The polite thing would have been to inform them both of his presence rather than eavesdrop on their private conversation. But before he could stop Corinne—or Rinny as he liked to call her—she was off and running. No, the best thing he could do, he'd decided, was to sit and wait her out. Besides, there were worse things than being stuck in the filing-room closet listening to Rinny let the Golden Boy have it.

Absently, Matthew rubbed his chest and thought to himself that there were much worse things. In fact, all things considered, he had the best seat in the house. Corinne always knew how to play the scene. And he'd been waiting for this particular breakup for some time now. Once Brendan was out of the way, he would finally have his chance. This time he was going to take it.

In the last few months, since he'd recovered from the bullet wound that had put a hole in his lung, Matthew Relic had learned two important things about himself. One: he was in love with Corinne Weatherby. Two: he would never again put off until tomorrow what could be done today. Life was precious. If that punk in the convenience store had taught him anything it was that.

Yes, he was definitely in the right spot at the right time. After Rinny was done dumping Golden Boy, she would need a shoulder to cry on. More than likely, the shoulder of someone who had a few extra tissues handy.

Matthew patted his breast pocket. He normally kept three tissues there. Today he believed he had four. A good thing, too, since Rinny tended to be extra watery.

He sat and waited for the rest of the scene to play itself out. She'd already given him the soulful goodbye. After that she would wipe the tears from her eyes. Then she would hold up her chin and carry her five-foot-nothing frame out of his office. She might turn dramatically for one final glance to show him what he was giving up, then in another second he would hear a slam signaling her departure and his release from the filing-room closet.

One. Two. Three.

Nothing.

Damn. She must be holding the dramatic pause too long. He counted again.

One. Two. Three.

Still nothing. Something must be wrong.

"I'VE GOT to go to the can," Brendan announced before Corinne could storm out of his office. Darn it, she had taken too long to wipe her tears in an attempt to save her eyeliner. She watched while he strolled out of the office and when she glanced down at her hand she could see the traces of brown eyeliner on her finger.

"Darn it," she shouted. "That wasn't in the script." She didn't even get to do the sultry look back. How was he supposed to spend the next two weeks pining for her, if he didn't have the sultry look back to remind him of all that he was missing? Well, she could only hope that the perfect suit, the ultimatum and the teary declaration of love would be enough to sway him to the right side of her particular force. What choice did she have?

This was the man she had fallen in love with. And since she'd been a girl she'd always believed there was only one true love for everyone on this planet. Once a person found that true love she had to grab him and hold on to him, because if the relationship failed, the couple was doomed to walk the earth in tragic loneliness forever. Or at least until eighty, when most people forgot about love and concentrated on soft food.

Knock. Knock. Knock.

That was odd; Brendan's office door was open. Who would be knocking? And why did it sound as though it was coming from behind her? Corinne whipped around and realized that the knocking was coming from the filing-room door.

"Ugh!" she growled as she threw open the door, utterly humiliated that she had an uninvited audience. That particular scene was supposed to have been a private show. "Matthew! What are you doing in there?"

He glanced down at the folder in his hand. "Uh, working."

"You bastard! You heard every word, didn't you!"

Since Matthew wasn't a great liar, he shrugged his shoulders and told her, "Yeah."

"Ugh! You don't even have the common courtesy to lie about it!"

"What's to lie about? You broke up with Golden Boy. I'm happy for you. You should have done it a long time ago."

"What do you know about it?" she hissed. "And if you heard the whole thing, then you will answer this question..."

"No, I wasn't out with Brendan and Marjorie from human resources last night. I'm Ole Relic, remember?" It was a nickname the others in their small company had dubbed him. Certainly, not the most flattering of names but Matthew had to agree it was rather accurate. He usually went to bed before ten on weeknights. He often did extra accounting work on the weekends. And on those rare occasions when Rinny could coax him out for happy hour, he only ever had one beer. Heineken. He liked the imported stuff. In summary, he was a C.P.A. who habitually carried extra tissues in his pocket. The very opposite of excitement and perhaps a little older than his thirty-three years would indicate.

"That rat!"

"Exactly," he agreed.

"That scoundrel!"

"Absolutely."

"That poor pathetic lonely man."

"What?"

Rinny reached out to touch his arm. She was a toucher. It was one of the things he loved about her. "Don't you see? He hides behind the lies because he doesn't think he has a choice. Deep down, he is this insecure boy who needs the presence of multiple women in his life to make him feel like a man. Virile. Get it?"

All Matthew got was that the guy she had just described sounded like a putz with a small...putz. "So where did he go?"

"He went to the, uh...the gentlemen's room."

Poor Rinny, probably not the way she planned it. "Did you even get to do the sultry look back?"

"I beg your pardon?" she asked, mildly offended.

"Come on, Rinny, it's me. When you used to visit me in the hospital you always flashed me the sultry look back right before you said good-bye. That look would follow me into my dreams. It's a classic."

"I don't know what you're talking about," she lied convincingly.

Matthew just shrugged his shoulders. In an effort to change the topic, he asked, "So, where are you going on your vacation?"

This topic made her slightly more chipper, and she put aside her pique. "Two fabulous weeks on Paradise Island in the Bahamas. Sun. Sand. And single," she finished on a slightly more depressing note. Visions of honeymoon couples frolicking about on the beach danced in her head. "I'm sure it will be mag."

"Yeah. Mag," he repeated. "What exactly does that mean?"

Poor Matthew, Corinne thought. She didn't know how it was possible, but he was even more lost than she was at this moment. Seeing his tie askew, she absently reached a hand up to the knot to tweak it straight. As she did, she studied the tie and the plain white shirt he wore with it. "It certainly isn't this tie. Really, Matthew, you've got to do something with your wardrobe."

He looked down at the tie she was arranging. "It's my favorite."

That made her snort. "And you need a haircut," she said, running her hand along his neck to corral the few stray hairs that lingered. His rich brown hair, a color he obviously didn't enhance, had always made her jealous. When he started to squirm, she pulled her hand away and thought that Brendan's hair was always perfectly groomed. He had a standing appointment with a stylist once a week.

Her name was Sherry. Sherry, who also happened to dance at a strip club for extra money on the weekends.

Corinne couldn't prevent the frown that she felt forming on her lips. She hated to frown. It always showed off the faint wrinkles at her mouth.

A tiny knock sounded behind them and they both turned to the open door.

"Is the coast clear?"

Corinne's assistant and good friend Darla poked her head into the office. The plump woman with the warm smile and bright eyes looked at Corinne expectantly.

"It's clear," Corinne told her.

"Well?"

"It didn't exactly go according to script."

"She didn't get to do the sultry look back," Matthew told Darla.

"Oh no. But that's, like, your heavy hitter. It's right up there with the playful pout."

"I do not have a playful pout. Or a sultry look back. You're both making this up."

They exchanged a glance that was all too easy to interpret, but Corinne didn't have the energy to fight them. "I just don't understand. Where did I go wrong?"

"Cheer up," Matthew said, bucking her on the shoulder. "And stop thinking about Brendan. You never know. You might meet some fabulous man and have a wild vacation affair."

She lifted her left eyebrow into a perfect arc over her eye. "Don't be ridiculous, Matthew. I am a one-woman man. One-man woman. Oh, you know what I mean."

Although, the idea did have a little merit. If she could send back pictures of her and some handsome stranger to her buddies in the office to view, and say Darla happened to accidentally drop one or two on Brendan's desk, well then that might be just the thing to push him over the edge. And if that didn't work, she could always literally push him over an edge!

"Uh-oh. I know that look," Darla warned, studying her friend's suddenly diabolical expression. "And it usually means involving me in one of your plots."

"Scripts," Corinne corrected. "And it does. I'm thinking about a whole new approach. What about jealousy?"

"You're always jealous," Darla reminded her. "You know, because Brendan's always messing around with other women behind your back?"

Corinne scowled at her alleged friend. "Not me. Him. What if I set out to make Brendan jealous? Of course, given my deep and abiding love for him, it would be almost impossible for me to flirt with another man..."

"You mean like what he's doing now with Marjorie from human resources?"

Matthew pointed to the scene just outside the door. Brendan was bending down to pick up a pencil Marjorie had accidentally tossed into the middle of his path, the whole time keeping his eyes pinned to her protruding breasts.

Matthew was amazed. "How does he manage to follow the conversation when he's got his eyes glued to her..."

Corinne shot him a menacing glare, and he quickly closed his mouth.

The bastard. The poor pathetic lonely... Nope, sometimes Brendan could be just a bastard. Corinne crunched her teeth together and squared her shoulders. She was going to be damned before she was made a fool out of by Marjorie from human resources. Calling upon all of her training, she focused on making herself taller with larger breasts. It was a visualization technique her seventh-grade acting teacher had taught her, and it had stayed with her ever since. Visualize yourself as you want to be seen and people will see it, too.

"Go get 'em, tiger."

"Give him hell," Darla added.

This from her cheering section. With the regal air of a queen she stepped out into the hall. Cubicles lined up along the hallway were filled with not-so-busy customer service representatives who had been enjoying the Marjorie and Brendan Show. Now that Corinne had added herself to the mix, the scene took on a whole new tension.

The question was, how did she want to play this particular act? All fifty employees of the small company knew about her on-again, off-again relationship with Brendan. Most thought he was playing her for a fool, but that was because they didn't understand him. Now here she was with her newest competition, who, if it was at all possible, was wearing an even shorter skirt than hers. The woman must have had her legs genetically engineered. It was the only explanation.

So did she go for catty? Explosive? Sorrowful and betrayed? Better yet, it was time for the old standby. She would play the bigger person. Not an easy task, considering she was playing the scene with an Amazon.

As cool as lemonade in summer, she strolled up to the couple standing too close together for company etiquette, and nodded her head. "Marjorie. Brendan. See you both when I get back." Enough said. She continued her march down the hall and out the door.

She didn't hear it, but she felt Matthew and Darla's applause accompany her all the way out the door.

IT WAS TOO EARLY for it to be hot. April was supposed to be about cool temperatures and soft breezes. But in New Jersey, when the humidity started to spike, anything was possible. Oh well, Corinne decided philosophically as she shucked her grasshopper blazer and noted the sweat stains, all the better to get her acclimated to the weather in the Bahamas. Still, it would have been the cherry on top to leave New Jersey while the weather was lousy for her two weeks of fun in the sun.

Dropping her suit into the dry-cleaning bin, Corinne checked the suitcase open on her bed one more time. Sundresses. Long flowy skirts. Strategic hip wraps. Three bathing suits. And SPF40 sunblock. For a redhead, frolicking in the sun did have its down side and its name was freckles.

The phone rang, and Corinne skipped through her condo to get to the kitchen before her answering machine picked up. When she missed the call by one ring, she decided she really was going to have to get another phone for her bedroom. But, since the only jack available was used for her modem, another phone also meant another line.

"Damn, I hate these things. Pick up dear. It's your mother."

Corinne cringed and considered playing not at home. She held her breath and waited.

"Damn it, Corinne, I know you're there. I can hear you breathing. Now pick up the damn phone."

Damn was her mother's favorite word. She said it was because back in the fifties it was the only swear word they would let a woman say on film. It sort of became one of her trademarks—the sultry eyes, the husky voice and the fact that she said *damn* before almost every line. The first few times it could be highly effective, but after the tenth or so *damn*, it started to lose its impact.

Knowing there was no way out, she picked up the phone. "Hello, Mother."

"Ah-hah, I knew you were there," Grace Weatherby said as if she had uncovered some dark and diabolical plot.

"I was in the bedroom," Corinne explained, not like that meant anything to her mother, who had only seen her condo once. And even that had been just a glimpse.

"I have tragic news. It's absolutely damning!"

Corinne waited.

"Your sister is refusing to go to the damn Cannes Film Festival. Can you believe it? I've told her, her only hope of winning an Oscar is if the critics start to see her as a serious actress. And she refuses to listen to me."

Serious actress. Myra? Corinne didn't think so, not when her last film had starred an alien and the film before that a ten-foot gorilla. "Myra is a Hollywood box-office star. Maybe she's content with that."

If you asked Corinne, Myra would have been content as a toll taker. Blessed with her mother's flaming-red hair and endless legs and her father's fine cheekbones and green eyes, she was destined to be Hollywood's girl for however long the ride would last. And, of course, the

Weatherby name didn't hurt. But Myra's heart was never really into it.

"The money isn't enough. Damn!" her mother exploded. "How long have I tried to instill in all of you that a Weatherby has won an acting award in each generation? Your father for best actor, me for best supporting actress, and even your brother managed to walk away with a Tony."

"And there was my plaque for employee of the month," Corinne added with her tongue in her cheek.

"Yes, of course," her mother agreed.

Corinne could almost hear her mother struggling to recall what it was that she did for a living.

"Darling?"

"Yes, Mother?" Corinne knew what was coming.

"What exactly do you do for a living?"

She was twenty-seven and had been working as a financial controller for the same company for the last six years. However, her mother chose to block such horribly dull thoughts as finance from her mind. So, each time Corinne mentioned her work, Grace would always have to ask the inevitable.

"I'm a controller, Mother."

"Oh, yes." Her mother sighed, even though Corinne knew she had no clue as to what that meant. "And do you still live in that...state?"

"Obviously, since I'm the one who answered the phone."

"Don't get fresh with me, young lady."

"Haddonfield is a nice town. And New Jersey is a fine state, Mother. It has mountains and beaches..."

"Please," her mother interrupted. "New Jersey is just that damn place right after you leave New York and are on your way to Hollywood. Anyway, the reason I called was to have you call your sister and tell her she must go to that damn festival."

"I can't call her. I'm about to leave for my vacation."

"Vacation!" her mother exclaimed, as if Corinne had somehow said the word *hell* instead. "Weatherbys don't take vacations."

They had had this argument before. "Most Weatherbys get three months off in between movies or productions. I have to go to work every day. I need a vacation."

A huge sigh, then, "Where are you going?"

"The Bahamas. Paradise Island."

"Dear, couldn't you have done better than that? Why, I can rattle off the top of my head at least fifteen more suitable islands."

"Paradise Island is in my budget, Mother." *Budget* was another word she knew her mother detested. Every once in a while Corinne liked to throw it into the conversation just to rile her. She could almost see Grace shuddering on the other end of the phone.

"At least tell me you're going with that nice man... what was his name? Brendan?"

Yet another reason why Brendan and she were destined to be together. Her mother loved Brendan. The one time Grace had managed to set foot in New Jersey, Brendan and Matthew had been helping Corinne move into her new condo. Her mother had practically recoiled at seeing Matthew, big and sweaty, wearing tattered jeans and a torn cotton T-shirt. There was such *plainness* about him, she'd told Corinne later.

But Brendan had made a big fuss over her mother, referred to her as Corinne's sister, then went on to list a few movies she'd starred in. Her mother had practically drooled over him.

It was that much harder to tell her mother that Brendan wasn't coming with her. "Not this time, Mother. He has to work."

Work on becoming an unattached man, that is.

"Well, you have a lovely time. And you'll call me when you return?"

"Yes, Mother."

"Damn, I hate good-byes."

"I'll call in two weeks." Corinne hung up the phone. "Or in two years," she muttered after she was sure the connection was broken. Sometimes her mother could be very draining, to say the least. Not that she didn't love the woman with all her heart, her father, too, it was just that they lived such a different life and believed in such different things that Corinne was never too sure how she came from them.

For one thing, the whole family mocked her idea of one true love. To them it was as foreign as domestic champagne. It was common knowledge that both her mother and her father slept with every leading person they ever starred with. Her mother could list ten true loves alone, and while her father's memory wasn't as good these days, given time he could list a handful as well. The only thing that had kept the family together was the fact that her mother and father had starred together in so many movies.

No sir, not for her. Myra had just broken off her fourth engagement. And her brother, Jeffrey, was working on his third wife. Corinne wanted something different for her life. She wanted stability. After all, she wasn't the most stable of women, so it stood to reason that she could only successfully fall in love with one man once. That man was Brendan. Now if only he would come around to her way of thinking, they would be a perfect match.

Even her family liked him. And Brendan liked the fact that he knew someone with "famous" connections. When they married, her parents would throw her a gala wedding to rival Myra's first wedding. Or almost-wedding. That particular fiancé she had left literally standing at the altar.

Regardless, she and Brendan would live happily ever after. Corinne was sure of it. If not, if she couldn't straighten his arrow, well then she was just going to have to deal with being single for the rest of her days, because she wasn't going through this agony again for anyone. And she highly doubted, anyway, that there was anyone else out there waiting for her.

Brendan was her mate. Her future. The other half of her soul. Without him she would live like old Miss Havisham of Charles Dickens fame. Alone. In a decrepit wedding dress and a room full of spiders. Forever.

Well, maybe not spiders. She didn't like them so much.

Ding-dong.

The doorbell startled Corinne out of her musings. That's strange. She wasn't expecting anyone. Instantly, her heart began to race. What if it was Brendan, she thought as she skipped through the house to her front door.

What if he had come to his senses? What if he was ready to give up all the other women so that he could be with her forever?

What if it was just Darla?

Corinne's face fell and her shoulders slumped when she opened the door to find Darla on the other side of it. "Oh, it's you."

"And hello to you, too," Darla greeted her with a sarcastic tone. "I figured you might be down so I brought some comfort food." She lifted the brown bag she carried in her hand.

"What is it?" Corinne asked.

"Brownies and vodka."

"Okay." Corinne took the bag and wandered back to the kitchen. "Only one brownie for me though. I've got to get this body into a bathing suit in less than forty-eight hours."

"Fine by me." Darla never had any problems with finishing off brownies. She made her way to the over-stuffed couch in the living room and sat down. "So Matthew told me that you told Brendan that if he doesn't give up the other women that it's *really* going to be over between you two. Is that true? This isn't just a ploy to get him to straighten up?"

"Matthew has a big mouth," Corinne said, returning from the kitchen with a tray of brownies, two martini glasses and a bottle of Cosmopolitan mix. She set the tray down on the coffee table, splashed the mix into the two glasses, then topped them with the vodka that Darla had brought. She handed a glass to Darla and lifted her own.

"Here's to a successful plan."

"Here's to your vacation," Darla said.

"Here's to my showing Brendan how much he'll miss me."

"Here's to looking good in your bathing suit," Darla said instead.

Corinne lowered her glass. "I'm not sensing I have your full support of my plan."

Instead of answering, Darla took a sip of her drink.

Gasping, Corinne stood up and pointed at her friend. "You *don't* support me," she accused her.

Wincing, Darla put down her glass. "I just don't understand what you see in him. He's been nothing but awful to you. I mean, Marjorie from human resources? Really! The only thing I can figure is he must be fantastic in bed."

Slowly, Corinne sank back down on the couch and took a sip of her drink. "I wouldn't know," she muttered.

"What!" Darla shouted, practically spilling her drink. "You're telling me you've never slept with him?"

"Do I look like the sort of woman who would sleep with a man while he was sleeping with other women?" Corinne asked, offended at the mere idea.

"No."

"When I'm finally with Brendan I want it to be special. I want it to be perfect. After all, he *will* be my first."

"First what?"

"My first lover," Corinne clarified.

Darla snorted at such an outright lie. "Are you kidding me? I know of at least one. What about Carlos?"

"Who?" Corinne asked, feigning ignorance.

"Carlos. The guy with hair and the motorcycle who you..."

"I know who Carlos is," Corinne snapped. "I'm just choosing to forget him. I'm revirginizing myself for Brendan."

Darla's brow scrunched. "Can you do that?"

"Yes, it's done all the time," she replied breezily. "I read it in a magazine. The point is, Brendan is my future. My destiny. My one chance to have the kind of life I've always dreamed of. If this trip away from him doesn't convince him of that, I don't know what I'm going to do."

"You could always, oh, I don't know, maybe find someone else," Darla suggested. "What about Matthew?

This may be out of left field, but I think he might like you."

Corinne dismissed that suggestion as if she hadn't even heard it. It was ridiculous. Matthew Relic liking her. Matthew Relic and her together. Impossible. It would be like putting the sun and the moon together.

"No. I refuse to turn into my mother or my sister or my father or my brother. All of them like to just flit and fly from one love to the next like bumblebees in heat. That is not going to be me. No, I've already decided that if things don't work out with Brendan, then I'm through with men forever."

Darla's eyes widened. "Wow. Forever? That's a really long time."

"Yes," Corinne choked out, feeling the fear building inside her.

"I think that calls for at least one more brownie."

Corinne did, too.

2

SHE STOOD OUT like a ripe plum in a white bowl.

Okay, so he wasn't the best at analogies but Matthew understood what he meant. With her red hair billowing out from underneath a grand straw hat, wearing her purple bathing suit and matching sarong, and stretched out in her chair on the powdery white sand, she was exactly as he had described. It just didn't sound as good when he tried verbalizing it in his mind. Good thing he'd tried this one out silently before he used it on her.

What he wanted to say was, boy she sure did look pretty. It was clear to Matthew, and surely to every one else on the beach, that Rinny was the most stunning girl on the stretch. In the clutter of people—most of whom were happy loving couples—camped out on the beach outside the Paradise Hotel and Casino, Matthew had no problem spotting his girl. If he were less of a practical man he would say that she had a powerful aura about her. Whatever it was, it seemed to attract him like a fly to... He should probably forget the analogies.

Flipping his beach towel over his shoulder, Matthew marched across the beach to her private camp. She had a beach chair on either side of her—probably to keep the happy loving couples at bay—filled with a radio, three books, enough sunblock to ward off a nuclear blast and finally her. She sat in the middle chair, her legs covered by the sarong she wore, her arms covered by the shade of her near-sombrero. The sunglasses that she sported were shaped like cat's eyes. Purple to match her suit. No doubt she had as many pairs of sunglasses as she had outfits.

His Rinny always knew how to put the package together. Standing before her, he waited for recognition from her that he was blocking her sun, but she was too covered in shade to notice. Beneath the glasses she must have had her eyes closed so Matthew decided to simply plunk his six-foot frame down next to her on one of the chairs. "Hi, Rinny."

Corinne had been dreaming. Brendan had been down on one knee before her with a ring box in his hand and a loving expression on his face. He had been promising her his love, fidelity and friendship for all the rest of his days. The dream was so powerful she could almost feel the tears well up in her eyes as they might if it were really happening.

Then suddenly, Brendan's face became Matthew's face with its deep-midnight-blue eyes and strong chin. And he was calling her Rinny. No one else called her by that absurd nickname. She wasn't even too sure why she allowed Matthew to continue to use it. Although the thought of trying to break him of the habit seemed exhausting. Matthew was like a steamroller. Slow. Plodding. Inexorable. And difficult to push off course. It made him a phenomenal accountant, but a bit of a bore.

"You asleep, Rinny?"

There it was again. This time Corinne did open her eyes and peer out over her sunglasses. There he was, plain as the sun, sitting next to her as if it were the most normal thing in the world. Matthew Relic was on Paradise Island. Somehow the two didn't seem to fit, but there was no doubt it was him.

"What are you doing here?" She wasn't too sure how she felt about his presence. Piqued because he had interrupted her vacation? Confused as to why he would follow her here? Or maybe a little happy to see a familiar face? After only two days, she realized that the next week and a half was going to drag with no one to talk to.

Most of the couples she met only stopped long enough to ask her where her husband was and if they wanted to get together for couples tennis. As soon as she explained that she was on the island by herself, they made their excuses and went on their way, absorbed with each other. She would have found the whole thing utterly depressing if she hadn't continued to tell herself that the purpose of this trip was to secure the very same happiness that these couples had found.

"Darla told me you seemed a little down before you left. She said something about a lot of brownies."

Corinne groaned, remembering how sick she'd felt the next day after eating all that chocolate.

"Anyway, she told me where you were staying. And I figured you would still be smarting from your breakup with Brendan, so..."

"Breakup?" Corinne interrupted. "We did not break up."

"Sure you did. I was in the filing closet, remember? 'No one is ever going to love you like I loved you.'" He changed the words, but the meaning was the same.

Corinne laughed her, oh-you-silly-boy chuckle. "Matthew, Matthew. You don't understand. That wasn't a breakup, that was an ultimatum."

"It was? It sure sounded like a breakup."

"It wasn't," she explained. "You see I left him to give him a chance to feel what it would be like if I *really* left him. No doubt right now, at this very minute, he is at home contemplating what his life without me will be like and he's wondering how he can get me back."

Right now, at this very minute, Golden Boy was probably at home romancing Marjorie from human resources. But Matthew kept that opinion to himself. He didn't want to hurt Rinny. He just wanted her to see that Brendan was no good for her, while he, on the other hand, was perfect. It wasn't going to be easy. He could see that now. He needed an angle.

"So what does he need to do? What is the ultimatum?"

She shifted a bit in her beach chair. "He needs to stop seeing those other women," she said tightly.

"You mean the ones that make him virile," Matthew added in an attempt to show her how misplaced her love was for that man.

"Yes. I'm enough for any man," she stated confidently.

"You can say that again."

"I beg your pardon?"

Leaning back on his elbows and stretching his bare legs out to the sun, Matthew took in the view of the ocean. The water spectacularly blue against the iridescent white sand, it was so beautiful it almost hurt. A little like Rinny when she got huffy.

"I was just agreeing with you."

"Hmm," she uttered, disbelief evident in her tone. "Somehow I don't think so. Well, if I'm so difficult then why are you even here? Don't tell me you came all this way just to cheer me up. Did you follow me down here for another reason, Matthew?"

It was pointless to lie. Even when he tried it, everyone could always guess the truth. "Yep."

"That's it? 'Yep.' That's the only answer I get? Sometimes you can be so difficult."

"I don't mean to be."

Corinne tried again. "Would you mind telling me why you followed me?"

"Well..."

"Never mind. I think I know," she stopped him. She tilted her head in his direction and gave him her, oh-you-poor-boy smile—which was only slightly different than her oh-you-silly-boy chuckle. "It's really no big secret. The truth is you have a little crush on me. Don't you?"

"I..."

"I don't mind," she offered gallantly. "Truly, it's not surprising. After all, it's only natural that someone like you would be attracted to someone like me. For one thing, we are complete opposites. That alone can be enough to stir someone's interest in another person. You see the qualities that you lack in the other and you want them for yourself."

He didn't think so, but rather than try to correct her assumptions only to be cut off again, he let her continue.

"The important thing is not to let it get out of hand. You know that I love Brendan and you know he's the only man I'll ever love."

"Why?" Matthew managed to toss into the conversation.

The question brought her up short for a second, but she recovered and quickly stepped up onto her Brendan soapbox.

"He's really a very sensitive man. I know sometimes he doesn't show it, but that's because of his insecurities. He feels he has to hide his true self. There's that and he's a talented salesman. Of course he has excellent fashion sense. And we're very much alike. We both enjoy the spotlight. We both play to the crowd. We understand each other."

"If he understood you," Matthew argued, "he would know that you're not the type of woman who would tolerate cheating."

"He's going to stop cheating. He knows he has to or he will lose me forever." There was a catch in her voice even as she said the confident words. "Would you want to lose me forever?" she asked him a bit frantically.

Gently, he shook his head, and said, "No. I wouldn't want to lose you forever. I guess I'm worried about you. What if he doesn't stop cheating? You're not going to stick around for that, are you?"

He would have to kill Golden Boy if he ever caught him with his pants down around his ankles with some other woman while he was married to his Rinny. And Matthew would hate like hell to have to go to jail.

Back to huffy in the blink of an eye, Corinne whipped off her sunglasses in a fluid movement and he could see how indignant she was. "Do I look like one of those pathetic women who would let her husband cheat on her?"

"No," he answered thoughtfully. "There's nothing pathetic about you, Rinny."

"Certainly not," she affirmed. "I promise you, I have no intention of sitting by and watching his roaming eye for the rest of my life. If he can't settle down, then we're through. Unfortunately, that means I will have to spend the rest of my life alone, and I would really rather it not come to that."

"Why alone? Why can't there be someone else?" he challenged.

Thoughts of her sister and all of her fiancés, and of her

brother and his two—soon to be three—wives and her parents with all of their paramours came rushing to the forefront of her mind. "Because it's not supposed to be like that," she stated adamantly. "There's not supposed to be scores of lovers in a person's life. Maybe there are multiple relationships, some that work and others that don't. But there is only one true love. The one that you're meant to be with. The one that makes your world complete. Sometimes that love only lasts for a day. Sometimes people never find it. Sometimes they find it but they let their day-to-day worries mess it up. Sometimes it lasts forever. You never know how it's going to end up. I'm lucky enough to have found my true love. If I'm not lucky enough to keep him...well, then I'll just have to live with the consequences. But it wouldn't be fair to anyone else who might want to be with me when I would know the whole time that they were just a substitute."

"I think you're wrong."

"What do you know about love anyway?" she asked impatiently.

"I know plenty," he said as he stared at the calm water. "I was engaged once."

Matthew had been engaged? This was news to her. Most people who met him automatically came to the conclusion that he was single. It was because there was something very solitary about him. When Corinne defended him to their co-workers, which she often did, she called him an independent spirit. Her colleagues said she was simply being kind.

They believed he was odd. Too staid. Too regimented. Too private. He ate the same thing for lunch every day— a bologna and cheese sandwich and a green apple. He wore a tie and suit every day, even on dress-down days when everybody else wore jeans. He always had a tissue and a pencil on hand and ready to lend. The man was as predictable as the turning of the earth. The girls in the office joked that being married to Matthew would be like being married to one of the presidents on Mt. Rushmore. In other words, not too exciting. No, no one ever seemed to question why he was single. And everyone took it for granted that he always would be.

Only come to find out that he was engaged. To be married. "Who was she?" Despite her best efforts, Corinne couldn't quite keep the incredulity from her voice.

"Her name was Debbie."

Wow, he thought. It had been too long since he thought of her. There was a time when Matthew used to think about her every second and what his life would have been like had she lived. But time had passed. His heart had healed. The memories would always be precious, but they weren't as keen as they used to be. And he had learned to love again.

"What happened?"

Corinne's curiosity was like a hungry animal that simply had to be satisfied, Matthew knew. She wouldn't stop until she had all the answers. "She died in a car accident two months before the wedding. Debbie was a schoolteacher, and there was a bad snowstorm and she wanted to make sure all the children got home safely, so she drove them herself rather than put them on the bus. They all got home, but she didn't."

It was tragic. A lump the size of a fist formed in her throat. "I'm so sorry."

He shrugged and sat up to take the pressure off his elbows. "It was seven years ago. I miss her, but I've moved on. And I believe that she would want me to find someone else. Someone who I could love as deeply as I loved her. She was generous like that."

The lump wasn't going away. Around it, Corinne choked out, "She sounds wonderful."

"She was. But after she was gone I never once thought that my life was over. I never believed that she was my only chance at happiness. Instead, I felt the opposite. I was reminded how dear life is and how I should always try to seize every moment. Somewhere along the way I forgot that lesson. I guess I've never been too good at seizing. It took a two-bit crook with a .38 Smith and Wesson and a craving for slushies to remind me." Reactively, Matthew reached up to rub his heart where he could still feel the residual pain from the bullet that had just missed that vital organ.

The scar was invisible behind the white cotton T-shirt he wore. But Corinne knew it was there. Odd, because he didn't seem like the type to be prudish about such things, but Matthew refused to let anyone see the mark that the bullet had left. He said it was a private matter between him and the man who put it there.

Corinne remembered that awful day as clearly as if it happened yesterday rather than several months ago. A police officer had shown up at the office with the news that Matthew had been shot during a holdup at a convenience store. Foolishly, Matthew had tried to talk the crook into putting his gun down, but the kid, doped up on PCP, had snapped and pulled the trigger. By the time Corinne got to the hospital, Matthew was nearly gone. The doctors said that although they had removed the bullet and closed the hole in his lung, he had lost so much blood in the process that they didn't know if he would ever wake from the coma that he had fallen into.

Miraculously however, just two hours later while Corinne sat with him, telling him about the plot of her sister's latest movie, Matthew had opened his eyes and smiled.

"I'm glad you didn't die," she blurted, abruptly returning to the present.

"Thanks. Me, too," he returned. "I'll never forget what you said to me in the hospital."

Corinne struggled to recall what he might be referring to, but she often said so many memorable lines. It would be nearly impossible to remember each and every one. It was one of the advantages of scripting most of the major events in her life. She always mentally wrote herself great dialogue.

"You said, 'Thank heavens, you're awake. I've few enough real friends in this world and I would just as soon not lose one.'"

"It was true," she reiterated.

"It was nice. It got me through, thinking that I had a friend like you who cared."

Now it was starting to make sense, Corinne realized. That's why he was here. It had nothing to do with a crush. It was out of some warped sense of gratitude that he felt for her because she was the only one who had come to visit him in the hospital.

Her vanity was somewhat offended. After all, chasing her down because he thought she was kindhearted wasn't nearly as flattering as being chased down because he thought she was gorgeous and sexy.

In an easy manner she laid a hand on his arm and gave him her let-me-give-you-some advice expression. "You just need to open up a little more, Matthew. People don't know you because you don't let anyone inside."

He never considered himself closed. He never thought about it one way or the other. He worked. He paid his bills. And he had his painting. By nature he liked solitude, but he didn't think he ever intentionally cut people out of his life. Then again, he never went to a lot of trouble to include them either.

"You know me," he reminded her.

And he knew why. It was because Corinne wasn't the type of person to wait to be let inside. She was the type who disregarded any barrier that got in her way. Even his stoic silence. He remembered their first meeting vividly.

They'd begun with the growing software company at the same time to establish internal financial controls— him as the auditor and her as the financial controller. She had waltzed into his office, and he'd immediately felt as if he were in the presence of a star rather than a serious businesswoman who worked with numbers all day. Her flaming-red hair had been loose about her shoulders; she'd worn a yellow sundress that flowed over her body like water over land, and from her wrist had dangled five gold bangle bracelets that clinked about and made music while she spoke.

We're both new which means we're bound to be friends. I'll meet you in the cafeteria for lunch. I prefer to eat around noon, low blood sugar and all of that, is that all right with you?

At the time, he recalled nodding, and then another gust of wind hit him in the face as she blew out of his office as dramatically as she had blown in to it. She'd left behind a lingering hint of her perfume and a hell of an impression.

They did eat lunch together that day. Mostly, Matthew sat and listened while she spoke about her plans for the company. He knew then that it was going to be his job to keep her in check. For whatever reason, that bologna and cheese sandwich and green apple had tasted better that day than it ever had before.

"Of course I know you," Corinne said, snapping him back to the moment. "After all, we work together. And you can't hide anything from me. Every thought you have is always written right there on your face. Come to think of it, you would make a lousy poker player. Be careful that you stay away from those tables when you go to the casino."

"I'll do that."

"It's not that I mean to be critical, Matthew. Truly, you are a wonderful man. And you deserve to have someone in your life. If you would behave more like a single man and less like a...like a..."

"Relic," he supplied.

"Yes...you would be amazed at the women who would come knocking at your door."

"But would any of them be you?" he muttered under his breath. Aloud, he said, "Thank you for the advice. Maybe I'll try that."

"Good," she said, pleased with her apparent success. "So what are you going to do now?"

"I was thinking of taking a swim."

"So you're staying?"

"If I wouldn't bother you."

"See," she pointed out. "That's another one of your problems."

"Another one?"

"You're too accommodating."

He thought he was just being polite. "But..."

She continued without interruption. "What difference does it make if I want you to stay or I want you to go? You probably paid just as much money as I did to get here therefore you have every right to enjoy your vacation. You shouldn't let me tell you what you can do."

"That's true...."

"You've got to learn to take what you want out of life and stop letting other people dictate your actions," she charged.

"Okay."

"You have to speak up, Matthew. Learn to just barge right in there with your thoughts and your wants. Let people know you're serious."

And he would have, too, if she hadn't kept rambling. After a few minutes he tuned her out, the point of her little speech having already been made. It wasn't the first time he heard one of Rinny's speeches, and he wasn't the only one ever to receive them.

Often, he could hear Rinny inviting people into her office, giving them a pep talk along with their assignments. She would listen to their woes and then pick that person up off the floor again with her cheerleader-like attitude.

Just another thing to love about her was her good and generous heart. It was a shame that few people ever understood her generosity. Most people got lost in the act she portrayed. They believed her to be whatever she wanted them to. Many were convinced she was simply shallow and self-absorbed.

But Matthew knew differently. He'd known it the minute he'd wakened from his coma and found her on the other side of his bed with unshed tears in her eyes.

"You've got to be bold," she continued. "You've got to be aggressive. And most important, you must always implement a course of action!"

Inwardly, he chuckled as her cheeks started to heat up

and her eyes began to take on a new glow. She wanted him to implement a course of action, huh?

What if he reached over there and pulled her off that chair, ripped off that silly sarong she had tied around her waist—no doubt to hide what she considered unsightly curves that he considered womanly—and kissed her until she couldn't see straight? That was a course of action he certainly wouldn't mind implementing.

It would shock her. It was something she would never expect from him, but he did have that side to him. It was one of the few things that Debbie had never understood about him. She had hated to be taken by surprise. For that matter she hadn't liked to be fondled much. She'd only made love with him after they became engaged, and then it had to be in a bed at night with lights out and her nightgown, if not on, at least close by. He'd loved her, so he respected her wishes. He had hoped that one day she would see that making love was about having fun and enjoying each other.

Making love with Rinny would be that. It would be that and a hundred other things as well. Intense. Hot. Exciting. Playful. He could see them together in his mind. A sudden surge of lust overwhelmed him and vaguely Matthew realized that the dunk he was planning in the ocean was suddenly becoming something necessary to cool his overheated libido.

"So I'm staying," he told her, not too sure where she was in her speech but wanting to at least make that clear. "And I'm going for a swim. Coming?"

Corinne was breathing a little heavily. Perhaps her speech had gotten a little out of hand. The good news, though, was that he had listened to her and had taken her advice. He was doing what he wanted to do and that was stay. Since it was what she wanted him to do, too, things had really worked out for the best.

"No, you go ahead. I'm not a real big swimmer."

This clearly confused him. "Why would you come to an island if you don't swim?"

Haughtily, she answered, "That's non-swimmer discrimination."

"It is? I thought it was just a question."

"Just because I can't swim doesn't mean that I should be denied the privilege of coming to an island. I like to look at the water. And maybe later, if I want to, I will sit by the pool, too."

He simply shrugged. "Okay."

"For now, however, it's getting late. I think I'll head back to my room."

"So, I'll meet you for dinner tonight. Around seven in the Pirate's Cove," he stated rather than asked. How was that for being aggressive and telling her what he wanted? Whether it worked or not remained to be seen.

He studied her face for a moment, and her expression was priceless. First, there was a little surprise at his forwardness, then a little outrage, then finally the realization that he had done exactly what she had instructed him to do. She was probably mentally congratulating herself on her success.

"Are you asking me to dinner?"

"I don't think I'm asking," he replied boldly.

She squinted her eyes at him, but then after a beat nodded her head. "Yes, I suppose I can meet you at the bar."

Corinne packed up her things and headed back up the beach. Matthew gladly watched the graceful movement of her hips as she sashayed her way to the hotel. Only the stupid sarong that she had wrapped around her waist prevented him from getting the full view. That was her sister's doing, he thought. Just because Myra was reed-thin, Rinny thought she had to hide the fact that she wasn't.

"You know, Rinny," he called out to her impetuously. "Your hips aren't all that big. You really don't need to cover them up with that sheet thing."

That being said, everyone within earshot immediately turned to stare at Rinny. And her hips.

Stiltedly, Corinne turned and shot death rays at him with her eyes. So powerful were they, he was relatively sure she would have killed him had she been a superhero. Turning away from him, her chin held high, she removed the sarong, as if to show her viewing public that she had nothing to be ashamed of, which she didn't, and stormed off. His Rinny always knew how to make an exit.

MATTHEW PLUNGED through the water and the gentle waves, finally diving beneath the surface of the clear ocean. When he came up he tried a few strokes, but instantly his lung started to hitch and his arm stiffened up. The one thing they never showed in the movies or on TV was how long it took to recover from a bullet wound. Most heroes just slapped a bandage on it and off they went. Here he was several months later, and he still wasn't up to snuff.

Don't regret getting shot, Matthew told himself as this time he took on the water a little more slowly. In retrospect it was the best thing that ever happened to him. If he hadn't gotten shot, he might never have woken up to the fact that time was passing, and he and Rinny weren't getting any younger.

After all, he was sure she wanted to have children. She

talked about having them with the Golden Boy, although he couldn't imagine him being anything more than an absentee father. Golden Boy was too self-absorbed for children. But Rinny would be an excellent mother, of that he was sure.

Yep, it was time for them to get started with their life together. All he had to do was convince her that she didn't love Golden Boy and that she did love him. Not an easy task, but not an impossible one. What had she said earlier, something about needing a course of action?

She was right.

He could always tell her how he felt about her. But after her speech about needing to open up to people, he had the sneaking suspicion that she had reduced his feelings for her to a minor crush, one rooted in the fact that she had been there for him. If he declared his love now, she might mistake it for misguided gratitude.

No, in this case, honesty was not going to be the best policy. Lousy poker face or not, he was going to have to give it his all to try and hide his true feelings for her. At least until he was sure that she could accept them for what they were.

There was always the friendship angle, but he'd played that card since the day he met her and all it had gotten him so far was her, well...continuing friendship.

Maybe he should tell her about Brendan and what a scoundrel he was and how Marjorie from human resources wasn't the first woman to make his eyes wander. No, any attack on Golden Boy would only lead to her leaping to his defense. Matthew wasn't up for another round of the poor-misguided-insecure-Brendan soliloquy.

So what was left to him?

Matthew flipped onto his back and began to back

stroke. The sky was a shade of blue that he couldn't quite label, but knew that when he got back to his condo in New Jersey, he would try to replicate it with his paints. He had no doubt he would fail. It wasn't that he was a pessimist. Just bad with colors. Not to mention he wasn't a very good painter. It was simply the process and its contrast to working with numbers all day that pleased him.

Then it clicked. The process. That was his course of action. He had to stop thinking about the end result and concentrate on the process. The end result was love and happily ever after. It was the ending that most people hoped for any time they began a relationship. But the process was the wooing. The dating. The flowers. The dinners. And the sex.

If Matthew couldn't get Rinny to fall in love with him, maybe he could get her to have an affair with him. Technically, she had broken up with Golden Boy, so she couldn't cry infidelity as an excuse. Then there was the added element of them being outside their normal realms on this island. Away from the office, their friends, anyone who knew them, they could be anybody they wanted to be.

It would be tricky. He would have to convince her that it would strictly be a two-week gig. No regrets or recriminations when it was over and they were back in the office. Of course, if he had his way there would be no "over."

Instead, there would be happily ever after and a nice house and babies and...Rinny.

It wasn't going to be easy. Pulling this off meant that he would have to be sneaky and manipulative. Two things he utterly failed at. But this particular poker game was for the jackpot. And he didn't plan on losing.

A vacation fling. It just might work.

3

TO TIE OR not to tie. That was the real question. Matthew was dressed in a pair of gray slacks to which he dared to add a soft-blue oxford shirt with a white collar. It wasn't his normal style. He preferred plain white. What with his lack of talent for color, it made it much easier to match his ties with his shirts.

However, fashion seemed to be important to Rinny. Or maybe not fashion so much as style. She was forever commenting on his absence of it. She'd given him this shirt as a Christmas gift last year so he had to assume it would meet with her approval. And there was the added fact that he simply wanted to wear it for her.

Besides, these were the islands. It was time to cut loose and live on the wild side.

He had gone so far as to roll the sleeves up to his elbows as a bow to the heat, but leaving it unbuttoned at the neck just didn't feel right to him. Again, he held the tie up against his chest. It was red. No doubt Corinne would have assigned some fancy name to the color, like vermilion or some such nonsense, but to Matthew it was just red. And red went with blue, didn't it? Oh well, it couldn't be that bad. Lifting his collar up, he secured the tie about his throat and tightened it. Then he tugged at it a bit, pulling it away from his neck ever so slightly.

Already, he felt a little wilder.

DECISIONS, decisions. Corinne stared at the five dresses she had laid out on the bed and contemplated each one as her potential dinner ensemble. One was too sexy, the other too loud. One was too girly and the other too prim. Number five it was. Really it was a combination of the four other problems, but to a lesser degree, so she figured she was safe. Slipping on a pair of panties, she stepped into the island dress.

It was a mesh of bright reds, yellows, whites and greens with huge blooming flowers all over it. As soon as she'd spotted it in the gift shop she'd known she had to have it. It tied about her neck leaving her shoulders bare. The flimsy island material overlapped, concealing her shape for the most part, but when she walked the material separated granting anyone watching the pleasure of a quick glimpse of thigh. A pair of three-inch strappy heels to give the effect of height, if not the reality of it, and she was ready for her date.

Evening, Corinne corrected. This was not a date.

Because it wasn't a date, she had no reason to want to impress Matthew with her new ensemble. Not at all. On the contrary she was going to have to be very careful not to flirt with him or smile too much. There was no reason to encourage his current crush regardless of its seemingly harmless origin.

But Corinne never went anywhere not properly dressed, and this evening would be no exception. She snapped up her matching red clutch purse and winced. The dress had been an indulgence, but the purse had been gluttony. She could almost feel the little pang of shock she was going to receive when she opened her credit card bill next month.

It always amused her when people assumed she was rich just because of her last name. Corinne would proudly point out that she had never taken a penny from her family. Instead she worked hard and invested well so that she was able to indulge herself every once in a while. Hell, if it weren't for her investments her family would be in debt up to their eyebrows.

Weatherbys know acting; Weatherbys don't know money, her mother would often quote. So it was left to Corinne to keep her family's fortune growing. Left to their own devices they would either squander their millions away or have it stolen by a corrupt accountant.

Not that they would care, Corinne thought sentimentally. Her family wasn't in show biz for the wealth. It was the attention they craved. The adoring fans, the boisterous crowds and the heat of the camera lights. The money was nothing more than a pleasant perk.

Not so for Corinne. Like everyone else who worked full-time, she needed money to live. She glanced at the perfect handbag that matched absolutely the vibrant red of her sandals. The purse was going to hurt. But the pain was worth it. And this was a vacation.

Tossing a scarf about her neck—a scarf she refused to acknowledge because it made the cost of the purse seem inconsequential—she left her room and headed downstairs to greet her nondate.

MATTHEW GLANCED at his watch again. He'd said he would meet her at seven. It was fifteen minutes after, so he figured he had another five minutes to wait. Had this been a business meeting she would have been downstairs at seven on the dot. She was obsessively punctual when it came to business.

Social events, however, were an entirely different matter. The Christmas parties. The office picnics. After-hours get-togethers. It didn't matter what the social occasion was, Corinne was always late.

Made for a better entrance that way, he knew. The fact that she was currently bordering on twenty minutes late meant two things—she considered this a social event, and her entrance was going to be spectacular. Matthew could barely contain the anticipation that was bubbling up inside his gut.

He checked his watch again. Twenty-one minutes late. Boy, she was going to look pretty.

"Hmm-hmm," she coughed delicately behind him.

Spinning around, Matthew felt his tongue pop out of his mouth. Probably not a suave move for a guy who was about to propose an affair, which was a very suave thing, he thought. As nonchalantly as he could, he drew his tongue back inside his mouth. A deep breath and he was ready to give her an appropriate compliment on her dress for the evening.

"Wow," he exhaled.

She smiled brightly, then frowned severely. "Ugh," she huffed.

Matthew reached up to make sure his stubby clipper-cut brown hairs were behaving themselves on the top of his head. He'd gotten the haircut per Rinny's suggestion, but the girl at Cuts-R-Us had gone a little overboard with the clippers.

However, it wasn't his hair that had earned her disapproval. Without hesitation, Corinne marched up to him and began to undo his tie. Although this was exactly how he planned to end the evening, Matthew wasn't so sure a public bar was the best place to get things started. But if she insisted, who was he to refuse her?

"I think you do this on purpose just to get a rise out of me," she muttered as she undo the tie and pulled it from around his neck. "This color red does not go with that color blue. Put it in your pocket."

He took the tie and shoved it in his pocket. He was about to outline his problem with colors in general, which also explained why people usually cringed whenever they saw one of his paintings, but she was still speaking. It wasn't polite to interrupt.

"I swear when we get back to New Jersey I'm going to take you shopping and show you how to dress. And if I have to show up every morning at your home to put you in clothes that match, that's just what I'm going to do."

Yeah, he was thinking along those same lines, her being in his house every morning to dress him. Naturally, it would be a help to have her there every evening to undress him. What with his pajama tops rarely matching his pajama bottoms. Inwardly, he smiled lasciviously.

As casually as if she'd been his wife for years, she reached up, no easy task considering their height disparities, and unfastened his top button. Smoothing the collar a bit, she sighed in resignation.

"I guess that's the best we can do for now. Remind me, however, that we need to go shopping in the gift shop. This is an island and you have to have at least one tacky island shirt. Why, look around you. Can't you see what all the other men are wearing?"

He saw flowers. He wasn't going to wear any flowers.

"At least you wore the blue shirt. It looks good on you," she decided. "It brings out the blue in your eyes."

"Okay," he muttered.

Really blue eyes. Deep, rich, almost vibrant blue eyes. Corinne had known Matthew for years, but she didn't think she'd ever paid attention to how truly remarkable those eyes were. Always so serious at work, he seemed more relaxed with her tonight. And that seemed to bring out a sparkle in his eyes. That along with the blue shirt and no tie...for the first time Corinne found herself acknowledging that Matthew Relic was quite a handsome man.

"Hello? Corinne?"

Breaking the contact and the sudden spell she had found herself in, Corinne tried to play it cool. "What?"

"You were staring at me," he said.

"I wasn't," she lied, with a little laugh to let him know how ridiculous he was being.

"Yes, you were," he insisted.

Silently damning him for his inability to let a white lie pass, she gritted her teeth and tried again, "No. I wasn't."

"Yes, you were."

Finally, Corinne snapped. "Okay fine, I was staring. If you must know I just never really noticed your eyes before. They're very nice. Very blue. Not traditional fair blue eyes, but a rich deep blue."

She thought he had nice eyes. The compliment made him almost giddy.

"You can be so stubborn," she accused, miffed that she was forced to confess something that any other man would have let slide. "Do you know that about yourself?"

"It isn't so much stubbornness as it is thoroughness," he tried to explain. "I like to have all the answers."

"Well, now you have them. Satisfied?"

No, he didn't think he did have all the answers. Certainly not to all the questions he had about Rinny. And he was a long way from being satisfied. But the fact that she liked his eyes was a nice start, he believed.

Just then the maitre d' interrupted them to let them know that the table Matthew had requested was ready.

The couple followed the man through the bar to their table. The restaurant was one of the more casual dining areas the hotel had to offer. Situated outside, it was actually roofed with colorful sun umbrellas that crowned every table. The area was lit with what appeared to be tiki torches, which Corinne assumed were something a little more technically advanced. And happy loving couples were everywhere. But this time it was okay. This time she was part of a couple...a couple of friends, that is.

Matthew held out a seat for Corinne and gently pushed her closer to the table. "Is this okay?" he asked as he took his own seat. "I thought that this might be more comfortable than the formal dining room."

"It's perfect," she assured him. And much better than having room service sent up to her room. She'd never realized that traveling alone could be so...lonely. With his presence, Matthew held the loneliness at bay. For that alone she was grateful to him.

A waiter came to take their drink order. Corinne began to explain with her hands the type of drink she would like. She moved them wide. "I would like something large, like in one of those bowls." She moved her hands lengthwise and added, "It has to be fruity and make my head spin." Finally she waved her hands about in a flourish and finished with, "Oh, and umbrellas. Make sure it has lots of umbrellas."

It took a minute for the waiter to get all that down, but eventually he turned to Matthew.

"I'll have a Heineken."

The waiter left and again Corinne sighed dramatically. "Oh what am I going to do with you, Matthew?"

He could think of a number of things, all beginning and ending in his bedroom, but he doubted that was what she meant. "I like beer," he said, because he knew she was disappointed in his very un-island-like choice in beverages.

"Yes, but you might like other things as well, but you'll never know unless you experiment."

The same could be said about her and her insistence that there could only ever be one man for her. "Tell you what. You can experiment and then let me know how it turns out."

"I'll do that. So tell me, if you're here then who is handling the preparation of the quarterly financials? You know we only have a few weeks after we get back..."

Matthew held up his hand, palm out, to indicate that she should stop. "No shop talk. That's my rule."

Her one eyebrow arched in a way that never failed to amaze him.

"You have rules for a vacation?" she asked mockingly. "Are there any others I should be aware of?"

Let's see, he thought. No shop talk, no Brendan talk unless he controlled it, no shopping—she'd find out about that one when she tried to get him to buy one of those island shirts—and no turning back. That last one was actually his own private rule. "I'll let you know them as they come up," he replied enigmatically.

Their drinks arrived. Hers a colorful bowl full of all sorts of exotic things that practically took up the entire table. His a simple frosty mug of beer. She dipped her head to take the straw between her lips, an action that drew Matthew's eyes to their cherry-redness and made beads of sweat pop out on his forehead.

"You can't tell me that you really wanted to talk about work. We *are* on vacation after all. I think it would be best to leave it behind us, back at the office where it belongs."

Corinne considered this. On the one hand, he was right, she didn't exactly want to spend her vacation talking about work, but on the other hand, that didn't leave a lot of other topics of conversation available to them. "But the financials..."

"Nope," he declared adamantly. "I'm not going to discuss it. It's funny, though, that of the two of us you would be the one to want to discuss the financials. I don't think anyone at the office knows how dedicated you are to your job."

She shrugged it off as if it didn't concern her. "No one takes me seriously because of my name."

"How come you never followed your family into acting? You're obviously a natural."

It was a question she had asked herself a million times. It certainly wasn't because she was shy or withdrawn. Like her family she loved the spotlight, but only on occasion. She wasn't obsessed with it like they were. And she also knew that the stable life she wanted to build for herself with her true love and her children would be easier to do in the real world rather than in the glitz and glitter that was Hollywood.

"I realized at a very young age that I wasn't as talented as my older brother, as beautiful as my younger sister, as glamorous as my mother, or as cute as my father. So I followed my natural talents with numbers and went into business instead. Much to my family's chagrin."

"The black sheep, huh?"

"Tell me about it," she laughed, although sometimes it wasn't always so funny to be the family outcast. "My mother is still insisting that there was a mix-up at the hospital. I think the only reason they let me attend family affairs is because of my red hair." So saying, she flipped her red locks off her shoulder.

"But you dye it red."

The waiter had chosen that moment to appear with his pad in hand ready to take their dinner orders. Red-faced, if not redheaded, Corinne gave her order through clenched teeth. Matthew in turn gave his order, and the waiter left.

Patiently, because she knew there was no malice in his comments, Corinne tried to explain some basic facts about women. "Matthew, you have to understand that women go to a great deal of effort and trouble to look good. However, most women, certainly me, like to give the illusion of effortless beauty. It does not help when you continue to point out what I'm desperately trying to hide. And how do you know I dye my hair?" she finished on a whisper, making sure the other diners couldn't hear her.

"The brown shows through at the roots every six weeks, then you go off to the salon and bang! You come back with red hair."

She could have done without the bang. "It's red," she insisted. "I just help it along a bit."

It wouldn't matter to him if it were purple. "I think you would look just as pretty with your natural color."

She rolled her eyes at him with an oh-what-do-you-know flair. "Brendan happens to like redheads."

And blondes and brunettes. Brendan liked women, period. But Matthew didn't say that. "My point is you don't have to do any of those fancy things to make yourself pretty. You're beautiful. And it's because of who you are."

"That's sweet, Matthew," she accepted, resting her hand on top of his. "But it's not reality. In this world a girl has got to compete with a lot of other beautiful women for the man she wants. My particular shade of brown...red...reddish-brown hair is a disadvantage."

The waiter returned and delivered their dinners. And this time Corinne was able to make the wide, long and fluttery, all in one fluid action, which was the waiter's cue to bring another fruity umbrella-filled bowl.

"You better watch those drinks," Matthew cautioned. "They can sneak up on you."

Corinne chuckled delightfully, an indication to him that the first drink had already caught up with her.

"Nonsense," she spouted, her head tilting slightly to the right. "They're ninety percent fruit juice."

But when the ten percent alcohol came in a glass the size of a fish bowl it wasn't so much nonsense as it was the beginnings of a massive hangover. Oh well, he decided, it might be fun to watch Corinne get toasted. It also might be a way to sneak past her stalwart defenses and learn what it was about Brendan that she was so in love with when all he had ever done was cheat on her.

"So," he brought up casually, while Corinne made slurping sounds as her straw made contact with the bottom of her first bowl. Obviously satisfied she had sucked the life out of it, she pushed it to the side and began on her second bowl. "Tell me what it is about Brendan that makes you believe he is your one true love."

Corinne lifted herself from her drink, no easy task as her head felt considerably heavier all of a sudden. Must be the island heat playing havoc with her sinuses, she concluded. Her smile beamed and her eyes twinkled. She knew this without checking her compact because it always happened to her any time she thought about Brendan. "There are so many reasons."

"Pick one," Matthew asked, not really up for a laundry list of Golden Boy's finest qualities.

"One," she repeated as if that task was virtually impossible. She plopped her hand on the side of her face with a smack. "Let's see. I think it would have to be the fact that he needs me so desperately."

"He needs you?"

"Yesss," she affirmed, her words beginning to slur slightly. "He's lost without me. I comfort him. I scold him. I push him. I nurture him. Without these things he would not be where he is today."

She sounded more like a mother and less like a lover, but Matthew held his tongue. Instead, he approached the topic from a new angle. "You do all of that for him. What does he do for you?"

This one stumped her. It shouldn't have. Corinne was positive that Brendan did a million things for her. Suddenly her memory was gone. She stared down into her fruity bowl. The second one was almost empty. Perhaps the drinks were the cause of her recent lack of memory. Or perhaps there wasn't anything to remember. She wasn't sure which.

Then it hit her. "He helped me move. Remember?"

Sure he did. Matthew had done all the actual moving while Golden Boy played kissy face with her famous mother. "Anything else?"

Squinting her eyes in an attempt to simulate concentration, Corinne forced her muddled brain to work. It was important to answer Matthew's question. Important for him to understand that she was emotionally committed to someone else, and important for her to know that she had made the right choice in her one true love. Finally, she had her answer. "He's going to give me the life I want. He's going to marry me and stay married to me forever. We're going to have a house and children and a dog. We're going to be happy. And normal. We're going to be very, very normal.''

Normal as opposed to odd, Matthew deduced, which was no doubt the life she'd experienced growing up in the Weatherby household. Still, he thought her answer didn't explain why she'd chosen Brendan. And now he knew without a doubt that she wasn't really in love with him. Perhaps she had convinced herself she was. Perhaps she wanted to be. Perhaps she thought he was the only sort of "normal" man her family would accept. But she didn't love him. If Matthew could convince her of that they might be in business.

The faint sounds of a calypso band began to float about the restaurant. Matthew watched with amusement while Corinne tried to pinpoint where the sounds were coming from. No doubt she thought the bells were coming from inside her head.

"It's a band," he explained. "They're playing on the other deck. There is dancing over there, too, if you would like to..."

"Oh, don't be ridiculous, Matthew. You can't dance."

"Actually I..."

"And I would never put you in a situation where you might feel awkward or uncomfortable."

"But the thing is..."

"I'm sure dancing ranks right up there with speaking in front of people for you, and I know how you hate that."

He did hate that. But he didn't hate dancing. However, in her state he doubted he was going to be able to convince her otherwise. "I think the best thing for you right now might be a walk on the beach anyway," Matthew suggested, hoping to sober her up a bit before he made his grand proposition.

Corinne stood on legs that wobbled slightly under her weight. "You're right. There is no way I could dance. Dancing would require too much...moving. Walking, however, that's a snap. See." She tried to show him by snapping her fingers, but her thumb kept slipping off her middle finger each time she tried.

"Come on, Miss Ninety Percent Fruit Juice," Matthew teased, clearly seeing she wasn't in complete control of her faculties. "The ocean air might just clear your head a bit."

He paid the bill and wrapped his strong arm around her waist, all but carrying her out of the restaurant and onto the path that led down to the beach. Once there he bent down to remove her sandals and watched in amazement as she shrank three inches. "You know, you don't need to wear these high heels to make yourself seem tall. I like you short."

"Short! I am not short!" she insisted. "I'm vertically challenged. The shoes are my crutch. Although I have to admit sometimes I find it difficult to walk in them."

Especially when you're snookered, Matthew offered silently. Tossing the shoes to the side of the path where he could find them later, he watched as Corinne wobbled down the beach to the water.

"Oh, isn't this glorious!" she shouted as she spread her arms out, her scarf blowing behind her like a set of wings. She looked as if she might, at any moment, lift off the ground and begin to fly over the water.

Yes, she was glorious. She was the most vibrantly alive woman he had ever known, and in return she made him feel more alive than he ever had before. Suddenly it occurred to him that he didn't know what would happen to him if she married Brendan. He feared his heart might actually break, and surely the pain from that would be worse than any gunshot wound.

Best not to let that happen, he decided. He had to stick to the plan. He would suggest an affair. Casual. Free. Hot and exciting. Then he would use that leverage in bed to convince her of the truth, that she wasn't in love with anyone other than him.

Sex would be a great deal of leverage with Corinne, he suspected. She wasn't the type of girl to sleep around. He knew that because she hadn't been with Brendan yet and she had been chasing him for over a year. And he couldn't imagine her being unfaithful to him as he'd been to her. She was way too softhearted for that kind of deceitfulness.

No, it didn't take a genius to spot that Corinne was a romantic at heart. It was there in the dresses she wore, the hats she preferred and the flowers she always kept on her desk at the office. Because of that, Matthew was certain she would only ever be with someone she believed she truly loved.

Or at least liked a whole lot. Matthew definitely fit that description.

Okay, Relic, he told himself. *Go for it.*

He was about to begin his pitch when he noticed an important detail. Corinne was nowhere to be found. He'd been lost in his thoughts for several minutes and now he couldn't seem to spot her.

Then he heard her giggle. He whipped around and saw her flat on her bottom. Apparently she had gotten too close to the water's edge and a gentle wave had knocked her over. Hell, in her condition a soft breeze could do the same.

"Corinne," he shouted, using her full name to secure her attention.

She turned and watched him as he approached. Vaguely, she wondered why he was walking lopsided, but then she straightened her head and in turn he straightened as well. Suddenly there were two hands under her arms, lifting her out of the sand. Since she hadn't bothered to put any weight on her two feet yet, she knew that he was supporting the whole load.

"Wow," she murmured, her eyes dropping to the roundness of his biceps that currently bulged against his shirtsleeves in an effort not to drop her. "Who would have figured that accountants could be so strong?"

Matthew was determined to view that as a compliment rather than an insult. "Stand," he commanded.

"I don't think I can. I can't feel my feet touching the ground."

"That's because they're dangling in the air."

"Oh."

With a plop, Matthew lowered her to the sand and voila, she was standing. He shook his head and decided that she wasn't in any state to listen to his proposal or to even understand what he was asking. It would have to wait until tomorrow.

"I think I'd better take you back to your room."

"No, I don't want to go back to my room," she whined.

Backing away from him, she held her arms wide and began to spin. Then she quickly realized that she was in no shape to spin. She stopped, only her head kept going. Finally Corinne used her two hands to stop her head. Once again the world came into a sort of hazy focus.

The water before her looked so refreshing. So inviting.

She turned to Matthew with a mischievous twinkle in her eye. "Let's go skinny-dipping."

He actually groaned. The thought of Corinne naked in his arms was enough to undo him, but since only one of them had any sense at the moment it was up to him to speak it. "You don't know how to swim, remember?"

Her hands were busy at the back of her neck trying to undo the knot and release the dress. It took a second, the one second before she would have shucked the dress entirely, for his words to sink in. "Oh. That's right. Skinny-dipping wouldn't be half so much fun if I drowned."

Maybe not for her. Matthew was still trying to deal with the concept that he had just lost his best opportunity to have Corinne naked and all to himself. But if his dear old mother had taught him anything, it was always to be a gentleman. And gentlemen did not take advantage of incoherent ladies.

No matter how much they wanted to.

Her arms suddenly heavy, probably from holding them above her head all this time, Corinne let them drop about her waist. Since the water was out, she searched the area for another form of entertainment. Her eyes fixed on Matthew. There in the moonlight with his strong arms and his big body, he looked almost as inviting as the ocean. Only much safer.

Yes, she concluded, with Matthew she was as safe as she needed to be. Taking one hand and placing it on her hip, Corinne began to sway toward him. In the process her hand slipped off her hip, so she had to stop and readjust it. It took a few tries, but she finally got there. "Have I ever told you how big you are?"

Another compliment? He wasn't sure. "Come on, Rinny. I'll walk you back."

"I don't want to go back. I want to stay here with

you." She reached up and circled his neck with her hands, combing her fingers through his hair as she did.

Think about Mom, he told himself over and over. Not only would it remind him what the right thing to do was, it would also prevent his lust from getting the better of him. Mom and lust simply didn't mix. Then he felt the tips of her fingernails gently scraping along the back of his neck and he knew if he didn't get them out of there soon, he was going to snap and end up taking her on the sand.

"And your blue eyes. I don't think I ever really saw them before tonight. I don't think I ever really saw *you* before tonight," she muttered.

"That's it. Let's go." In one smooth motion, Matthew bent and lifted her into his arms, one arm cradling her back, the other under her knees.

"Weee!!!" she screamed, thinking she was on some kind of ride. "Look at me, I'm Scarlett O'Hara. Oh, what did she know? Ashley was nothing but a big sissy. Rhett was the real man."

Matthew turned his face toward her and smiled. There she was, cradled in his arms, as snug as if she were a baby. Her face was awash with a red flush and her green eyes twinkled under the moon. Damn, he loved her.

Hiccup! Achoo.

"Bless you," he said.

Hiccup!

Oh no, he sighed. He was sensing a pattern.

Achoo.

"Bless you."

"Thank you." Hiccup. Achoo.

Ironically, and unfortunately for him, it was the first

time he could remember not having any tissues on hand. "Bless you," he repeated.

The journey back to her room was fraught with adventure. First they had to stop while she picked up her shoes, all the while refusing to leave the shelter of his arms. Then there was the group of people in the lobby he had to carry her past, making sure her tiny feet didn't clock anyone in the face. During all of this she continued to hiccup and sneeze to a chorus of "Bless you," each time causing her body to jump and him to almost drop her.

Finally, they reached her room. In the hall, he set her down carefully, her back to the wall for support. But as soon as he released her, her knees buckled and she slid down the wall until she hit bottom. Her bottom.

"The key, Rinny?"

Bewildered, she looked up at him. "Have you gotten even bigger?"

He spotted a handbag that fortunately she still had clutched in her hand. He reached down and opened the purse, ruffled through her compact, her lipstick, her eyeliner and her extra little bottle of perfume, until he found the plastic key. He unlocked the door and threw it open. Then he bent down to retrieve his date.

"Up, up, up and away!" she sang, as he once again lifted her into his arms. "You are the strongest, the smartest, the handsomest manest ever."

That was definitely a compliment. Matthew searched her eyes hoping for a hint of truth in them, a sober thought that had escaped past her alcohol-laced tongue.

"Oh, Brendan." She sighed.

So much for the compliment. Irritated, Matthew took the last few steps to the bed and dropped her.

"Oops," she screeched as she bounced on the springy mattress.

Bending down over her, his arms on either side of her shoulders, pinning her to the bed, he forced her to see him. Really see him. "My name is not Brendan!" he shouted uncharacteristically.

Taken aback, because even in her muddled state Corinne knew that it was a rare thing for Matthew to raise his voice, she said, "I know. You're Matthew." She put her finger on his chest. Then turned the finger on herself. "And I'm Corinne."

"Say it again," he ordered. "Who am I?"

Uh-oh, he must have had too much to drink if he couldn't even remember his own name. Patiently, Corinne said again, "You are Matthew."

"That's right. And tomorrow when you wake up it will be with my name on your lips. And my taste." He closed the distance and captured her lips.

Corinne was too shocked to do anything but hold on for dear life. She clutched at his arms while his mouth ravaged hers. She felt his tongue sneak past her teeth. She felt his breath fill her mouth. Then she felt his tongue dancing with hers, encouraging her to play and explore and she was helpless against the need that told her to do just that.

Matthew tugged at her lips. He drew her tongue back into his mouth and felt her response as her nails began to dig into his shoulders. Kissing her was everything he knew it would be. Hot, intense and devastating.

A boy must grow to be a gentleman.

The image of his gray-haired mother appeared in his mind, and he was grateful for it. He didn't want their first time to be like this. He wanted more control over the situation and right now he didn't have it. In fact he was only a breath away from ripping Corinne's dress off and sinking deeply into her womanly warmth.

But not like this. When they came together for the first time Corinne would be sober and completely aware of what was happening to her and who was having her. And Matthew would know that it was him she truly wanted.

With more willpower than he realized he had, Matthew released her and took two definitive steps away from the bed as he tried to catch his breath.

"Matthew." She sighed, leaning on her elbows, seeming to sway back and forth on the bed. "Oh my." Then she collapsed, her arms giving out, and she fell back into the comforter and pillows.

This was his cue to leave, but Matthew couldn't help but think that she would be awfully uncomfortable if she woke up the next morning still dressed. The question was, did he have enough willpower left to get her undressed without peeking?

The answer—no.

At least he was being honest with himself. Instead he pulled the comforter from one side of the bed and tossed it over her so that at least she would be tucked in and cozy in the air-conditioned room. He had turned to leave when he heard a faint sneeze from under the cover.

"Bless you," he offered again. "And goodnight. We have some unfinished business. But we'll deal with it in the morning."

The only response he got was a faint throaty sigh that most people would define as a snore.

Somehow Matthew knew that Corinne would never own up to snoring.

4

"Oнн," she moaned. "Ohhh," she moaned again. "Ohhh."

Wait, wait, wait, she told herself silently. The moaning only made her head hurt worse. If such a thing were possible.

Slowly coming to her senses, Corinne took a minute and attempted to get her bearings. For one thing, she knew she was sprawled out on the bed in her hotel room. She recognized it as such because all her clothes were still strewn about the furniture in the room.

That was a good thing.

But her next impulse was to reach out her hand and search for the presence of a stranger next to her in the aforementioned bed.

That was a bad thing.

She couldn't say why, but she was pretty sure she had gotten hot and heavy with some man last night. Whoever he was, his kiss had followed her into her dreams and played all sorts of havoc with her libido. She could still taste him on her lips.

But her hand's search revealed nothing. Which could either mean he was a jerk and had snuck out before he had to face the music, or he was a terrific guy and had decided not to take advantage of a woman in her less-than-sober condition. For now, she was going with the terrific guy scenario. It seemed to play right in her head and gave her less to fret over this morning.

Since she was currently handling all the physical pain she could at the moment, it was best not to add emotional pain to that as well.

The next step was to open her eyes. Her eyes! Damn, she'd forgotten to take out her contacts. Attempting the impossible, she tried to pry her eyelids open. They cracked open to mere slits and she could hardly see through the red haze. Bolting out of bed, a feat that she knew she would pay for in the near future, she rushed to the bathroom.

Her reflection in the mirror was a mere blur, but out of long habit her fingers knew what to do. Removing the green-colored lenses, she dropped them into the already prepared solution that she had left out on the countertop and took stock of the situation.

Her lids were puffy. There were red rings under each eye, and her naturally hazel eyes, formerly vibrant green, were so bloodshot she looked like an alien creature.

Then it occurred to her that she was standing.

"Ohhh," she groaned as the pain from rushing out of bed finally caught up with her. She knew she had to return to the prone position, but first she managed to soak a washcloth in cold water. Hobbling back to the bed, she fell into it once again and placed the cold compress over her eyes hoping to reduce the swelling.

What had she done? She remembered a fruity drink in a large bowl. Vaguely, she remembered a second. Two drinks didn't seem like enough to be paying this awful price. But here she was, practically numb with a hangover and a lot of missing time to piece back together.

The best place to start was at the beginning. Matthew

had asked her out for dinner. Well, actually he had told her he was taking her to dinner, which was very high-handed of him really.

Matthew. That's right. Matthew was on the island. He had taken her to dinner and then…she struggled with the next event in the timeline for a moment, but an image of the moon over the water and sand under her bare feet flashed in her mind.

The beach! Vaguely, Corinne remembered a sense of floating, which had to have been a part of her dream as it seemed highly unlikely that she could have done any floating in the water considering the fact that she couldn't swim. Was it possible that Matthew had carried her? That, too, didn't seem very likely—way too roman-tic an image to associate with someone like Matthew—but since she had no other explanation as to how she had managed to make it back to her room, she decided to ac-cept that as fact.

And there was something else. Something important. Something earth-shattering in fact.

"Oh, my goodness," she gasped. "He kissed me!"

Yes, she was sure of it. The image of his face moving in closer and his lips touching hers was impossible to for-get. Worse, she remembered liking it. Loving it even. His one kiss had done more to spin her head than the two fruity drinks combined.

But what happened after that? Considering this was Matthew, it was a good bet that she was dealing with the terrific guy rather than the jerk. No doubt he had tucked her in and taken his leave. Hesitantly, gingerly, she lifted her head and stared down at her body. The dress from last night was still there. She sighed with relief and let her head fall back on the pillow.

"Ohhh," she whined, as the agony rippled through her body at even that slight movement.

Okay. So Matthew had taken her to dinner and kissed her. That wasn't so bad. Nothing she couldn't deal with. True, he had a crush on her, born out of some kind of misplaced loyalty. And unfortunately, kissing him back—and she was pretty sure she *had* kissed him back—wasn't going to do anything to cool that crush.

Poor man. He couldn't help but be captivated by her. To him she was probably everything in this world that was out of his reach. So naturally, he tried to reach for it. She couldn't blame him for that. As long as he understood who held her heart, a fact she had made infinitely clear, then she couldn't be responsible for any hurt feelings.

Belatedly, she wondered why he had kissed her. Had she asked him to? Impossible.

Knock. Knock. Knock.

"Ohhh."

Knock. Knock. Knock. "Rinny, are you awake?"

There was a solid door and several feet between them, but still, his shout seemed to penetrate her skull and rattle her brains.

"Yes," she whispered back so he would stop shouting.

Pound. Pound. Pound. "Come on, Rinny, wake up. I want to talk to you."

Evidently, he didn't hear her. Rolling out of bed, her now-warm compress falling at her feet, she staggered to the door, stretching out her arms in front of her to help her navigate. Not only did her contacts color her dull hazel eyes to a bright forest-green, but they also performed this other useful task of allowing her to see. Corinne found the door handle and opened it.

"Whoa!" he remarked.

Somehow she got the feeling that this "whoa" was miles away from the "wow" she had elicited from him last night.

"Rinny, are you...I mean, can I...I mean... What happened to your eyes?" Matthew had intended to ask if he could lend a hand, or at least a few aspirin, upon seeing her condition, but through the redness of her eyes, he distinctly saw a hazelish-brownish color rather than the green he was accustomed to seeing. Surely a hangover couldn't do that.

One more secret revealed. Not what she needed during the worst hangover of her life. "You do realize if you discover any more of my secrets, I am going to have to kill you," she muttered as she turned away from him and hobbled back into the room. "Nothing personal, you understand."

Matthew followed her and shut the door behind him. Corinne winced at even that small sound and shot him an angry glare. Considering the appearance of her eyes right now, she imagined her glare was rather intimidating.

"Sorry," he apologized for the door. "So tell me what happened to your eyes?"

"I left my contacts in too long," she explained.

"And that turned them brown? Seems like a hell of a price to pay."

"No, that didn't turn my eyes brown," she snapped waspishly. "My eyes are hazel. I wear colored contacts to enhance the green."

He saw more brown than green, but he kept that to himself. He did add, "I think hazel is a very pretty color."

"You would. Now, I assume you have some reason for visiting me at this hour? Or have you just come to revel in my agony? And if the words *I told you so* fill this room in the next few minutes, I won't be responsible for my actions."

Actually, he had come to see if she would consider sleeping with him, but given her present condition he decided that question would have to wait. "If I can't say I told you so, how about I say I warned you about those fruity drinks. They pack more of a punch than you realize."

"Punch? I feel like I've gone ten rounds with Muhammad Ali. He's the boxer, right?"

"Yeah." Matthew smiled. "Why don't you hop in the shower? Keep the water ice cold. It helps. Then I'll take you to breakfast."

The thought of food was enough to send her stomach rolling. "I don't think I'm up for breakfast."

Matthew moved farther into the room and stood behind her. "Really what I want to do is talk. About last night." He paused for a few beats waiting for a response. When none came, he began to wonder if she even remembered what happened last night. "You do know that we kissed last night, Rinny?"

Spinning to face him, her face ashen, Corinne gulped heavily. "I'm going to be sick." In a flash she darted off to the bathroom.

He scratched his head and thought to himself that vomiting definitely wasn't a good sign. Of course, maybe it wasn't the memory of his kiss that had sent her fleeing. At least he hoped it wasn't. He followed her to the bathroom and soaked a washcloth in cold water. Kneeling beside her he placed the cloth on the back of her neck and held her forehead in his hand while she emptied what was left of the fruity drink into the toilet.

When the violent spasms ended, Corinne fell back

against the tub an exhausted wretch. She stared at him in amazement as Matthew calmly stood and filled a glass of water for her. "Why are you still here?" she croaked out past her sore throat.

"Because someone has to help you through this."

"But this is horrible. I look horrible. I smell horrible. You've just seen me at my absolute worst. Why aren't you running for the door?"

He handed her the water, which she took gratefully and gulped down quickly. "We're friends," he said as if it made all the sense in the world. "Friends are there for each other regardless of what you happen to look like at the time. Remember how I looked in the hospital? It didn't stop you from visiting."

Yes, she remembered how he looked. White. Weak. It had scared her. For as long as she had known Matthew he'd always appeared sturdy and strong. He was a rock. A brick wall. The tide. He was all things unshakable and predictable. But when she found him lying in the hospital in a white gown that matched the color of his skin, she remembered thinking that he was capable of doing the most unpredictable thing...like dying.

She gazed up at him to confirm that he was still very much alive, and didn't dwell too long on why it was so important to her that he be that way.

"You can take your shower now. Remember, cold water. Then I'll take you out for eggs, toast and black coffee. There's nothing better for a hangover."

"You sound as if you speak from experience," she commented while she waited to see how the mention of eggs was going to play with her stomach. Not too bad. In fact the idea of food was starting to sound appealing. Perhaps she was on the mend.

"I went to college."

"Enough said."

He reached his hand out and she grasped it. Immediately she felt his sturdiness. His sneakered feet were firmly planted on the ground while he lifted her to a standing position. "You're being awfully nice."

He wished there wasn't such suspicion in her voice. Instead of answering her, he patted her cheek. "Take as long as you need."

An hour and a half later Matthew was considering that maybe he shouldn't have told her to take as long as she needed. After all, this was Corinne Weatherby, one of the most high-maintenance women he had ever met. God only knew what concoctions she was applying to her hair and face and...her body.

Matthew shook off the image of her naked behind the door slathering sweet-smelling lotions all over her body. It didn't seem fair to be having sexy thoughts about her when she was clearly not feeling up to her usual snuff. So instead he tried to think about what he was going to have for breakfast. Only, that was starting to make him really hungry.

Fifteen minutes ago the bathroom door had cracked open, and for a second Matthew thought he was finally going to get fed. But all she had done was instruct him on what clothes to pass through the crack.

Unfortunately, as he passed her the jean shorts and bright green polo shirt, along with a pair of lacy white panties and a matching bra, the sexy thoughts returned. This time, however, he let them linger because the stray images of soft flesh and fresh scented skin helped to alleviate his hunger.

As another five minutes passed, the hunger was starting to win out again.

Men were such basic creatures, Matthew realized.

A noise captured his attention and he hopefully raised his gaze to the bathroom door. What emerged was an absolute work of art. Her previously frazzled hair was now a playful nest of curls piled on top of her head. Her puffy hazel-brown eyes were now covered with a pair of dark round sunglasses. Her lips were painted. Her skin color was smoothed out. Her pert little figure was enhanced by the slimming shorts and the bright green shirt. The woman before him now bore no resemblance to the pathetic little waif who had collapsed on the bathroom floor.

"How do you feel?" he asked because it was plain to see that with Rinny, appearances were deceiving.

"Better," she admitted. "The cold water helped. I actually think I'm hungry."

"Good." He offered his arm and after a second she took it.

IT SHOULD HAVE mortified her to even look at him knowing what he had done for her that morning. No one had ever seen her so bare before. Certainly, she had never shown that side of herself to Brendan. Instinctively, Corinne knew that Brendan would have a hard time dealing with sickness of any kind. He wasn't necessarily the nurturing type.

But Matthew had handled the whole incident as calmly and patiently as he would have handled an audit. And because he had been so nonchalant about everything, she didn't feel half as awkward as she should have. Having him there, holding her while she got sick, seemed almost natural.

"I'm glad I got sick with you," she announced as they rode down in the elevator.

Matthew turned to her with a quizzical expression.

Then she realized how her words had sounded. There she went again, not preparing her lines before she spoke them. It inevitably got her into trouble when she did that. "What I meant to say was that if anyone had to see me like that, I'm glad it was you."

He smiled.

"Not that I ever want to do that again mind you. I think for the rest of the trip I'll stick to the occasional glass of wine. It's awful being so out of control. And I hate the idea that I can't remember certain things."

The elevator doors opened and Matthew let her pass. He then ushered her to the hotel dining room where they were serving brunch until one that afternoon. It was close to noon and he was glad to see that they would have the dining room mostly to themselves.

It was his intent to lay his plan out to Corinne this morning, and it was highly possible that she might not take to the idea and cause a scene. Matthew wasn't very good with scenes, but Corinne excelled at them. If one were about to happen, then at least there would be a relatively small audience. Sort of like an off-off Broadway production.

They were seated and delivered their orders to the waitress. When the eggs came out, Corinne dove in with relish and after the coffee and two glasses of orange juice she could finally say that she felt human once again.

Matthew, on the other hand, was having a hard time concentrating on his food. He'd gone over his speech a thousand times last night, but now when he needed to deliver it, he couldn't recall a single word.

There had been several reasons he had planned to give Rinny. Reasons why it would be in her best interest to sleep with him. At three in the morning those reasons sounded logical and convincing. But in the light of day they sounded cold and unromantic. And a little silly.

Oh hell. Sometimes he wished that he were a different sort of man.

Brendan, he mused, would probably have no problem spouting out smooth words with which to seduce Rinny. A man with his lines would no doubt have her on her back in hours with a few choice comments about her hair and her eyes and how she resembled the tropical flowers outside or some such nonsense.

Then again, Brendan hadn't succeeded in seducing Corinne in all the months they had been dating. Maybe Corinne wasn't the sucker for soft words and sweet lies he thought her to be. Maybe logic would work where flattery had failed. The bottom line was, Matthew wasn't going to change his inherent nature over coffee. He was who he was.

"I think we should have an affair."

Her fork was halfway between the plate and her mouth. His words seemed to freeze the utensil in midair. Or perhaps it was her shock at hearing those words that had done that.

It hadn't come out exactly as he had planned. In his speech last night he had done some—not a lot, but some—leading up to the proposal. Matthew just wasn't any good at speeches.

Carefully, Corinne replaced her fork on her plate before she dropped it. Sometimes life didn't follow the script. Sometimes the other actors in her world decided to improvise and throw her a huge curve ball. This was one of those times.

She laughed nervously. "I'm sorry, I don't think I heard you right. What did you say?" She knew exactly what he said. She was simply giving him the opportunity to retract his ridiculous proposal.

"I said I think we should have an affair. With each other," he added in case that had been unclear.

"Let the record show that I tried tact," she muttered under her breath. Then to him she said, "Are you crazy!"

It wasn't totally out of the realm of possibility. After all, he had flown hundreds of miles, blown his vacation allowance, and now was offering an affair to a woman who had told him on numerous occasions that she was in love with another man. She was right. It was crazy.

But then the kiss they'd shared last night replayed through his mind. He took into consideration that she had been drunk at the time, but there had been a chemistry between them that had not surprised him. He wondered if it had surprised her.

"Hear me out," he began. "The two of us are here together on this tropical island..."

"Only because you followed me here," she interjected.

All it took was a raise of his eyebrows to let her know that she was not abiding by his first rule to hear him out. Corinne leaned back into the chair with her arms crossed over her breasts. "Go on."

"Thank you. Anyway, your ex-boyfriend is currently mixing it up with another woman in the office. Were you to have an affair with me that would go a long way toward showing him that you're not going to just sit back and accept his infidelity."

"You want me to sleep with you so I can get back at Brendan." She had intended the statement to sound ludicrous, but as soon as it rolled off her tongue she concluded there was a certain kind of warped logic in it.

"You did tell Darla you were thinking about a plot to make him jealous."

A few pictures. A few lies. A little play-acting. Not an actual affair, Corinne remembered. "Matthew..."

"I'm not done. An affair would be wild and exciting and unpredictable. All those things that you love about life, but you never really seem to take part in. This would be your chance to do something out of the norm."

Corinne shifted in her seat. She took mild offense at the statement that she never did anything wild and unpredictable. She was, after all, a Weatherby and they excelled at exciting. But when she looked back over the last few years she couldn't recall one thing other than falling in love with Brendan that had been remotely daring. Strange. Was she really that boring?

"Not that I think there's anything wrong with your life. You work hard. You are a good friend. You do the story hour at the public library every Saturday."

"You know about that?"

Matthew smiled. He'd seen a poster with her name on it in his neighborhood. He had gone to see the performance, but stayed in the back so as not to distract her. It had been brilliant. Little Red Riding Hood had never been so full of vigor and her Wolf had been positively sinister. "I know a lot about you."

Contemplating that statement as well as his proposal, Corinne began to get nervous that she wasn't tossing her glass of orange juice in his face, which is exactly what he deserved for proposing something so outlandish. But her head still hurt slightly, the juice did taste good and she didn't have the energy to order another one. "Go on."

Encouraged by the fact that she hadn't stormed off, thrown food or slapped him across the face, Matthew proceeded with his arguments. "You can't deny that there was a chemistry between us last night."

"Yes, but I believe in this case what you call chemistry is more commonly known as alcohol. To be precise, rum."

"I wasn't drunk. And it was more than the rum. Admit it."

It was a risk, he knew. Just because he had been blown away by their kiss didn't mean she had. He was banking that nothing that felt so good to him could have been all bad for her. And he had to hope that if it were true, she would be honest about it.

Matthew had a point. That kiss had practically knocked her out of her dress. In truth if he had been any other sort of man, he could have wooed her into bed, and as drunk as she was and as excited by him as she was, she probably would have followed.

Instead, he'd waited until she was sober, then asked her to go to bed with him. That alone was a tribute to the type of man he was.

"Let me sum up," she counted. "Inciting Brendan to jealousy, the thrill of the unpredictable and the chemistry we have between us—for these reasons I should agree to sleep with you?"

Matthew recounted the reasons on his fingers. When he looked down at his hand he saw three fingers, but he was sure last night there had been four. Oh well, he was going to have to take his chances with three. "Yes."

Time passed while Corinne deliberated. First she tilted her head to the right. Then to the left. Corinne was the only person he knew who could talk to herself and literally display the whole conversation on her face as she did.

After what seemed like an eternity, she took a deep breath and said, "I'll consider it."

For the time being, he was satisfied. "Are you finished with breakfast? We could head down to the beach."

The two of them sat in side-by-side lounge chairs and stared out at the ocean. Corinne pretended to read her paperback, and she knew that beside her Matthew was only pretending to sleep. No doubt he was anxiously awaiting her answer.

Make love to Matthew.

For the life of her she couldn't fathom why the concept of sex with her very good friend didn't repulse her. She was supposed to be a woman in love. The mere mention of any other man taking what was rightfully Brendan's should have appalled her. But it was so hard to take offense with Matthew. He was too good. Too honest. His proposal had come from the heart. He sincerely wanted to make love to her for no other reason than that he wanted to.

Perhaps she should consider denying him for that reason alone. Corinne didn't want to encourage his crush. She didn't want to break his heart. The thought of him crying as she walked down the aisle to meet another man bothered her on a very elemental level. Matthew had suffered enough pain in his life. The loss of his fiancé, the bullet that had nearly taken his life. She didn't want to add to his pain.

On the other hand, the man had had a brush with death. After waking up from a coma, the first thing he wanted to do was make love with her.

Well, actually not the very first thing. The first thing he'd asked for had been a glass of water. Then he'd wanted to know the time.

But after time and water she was a close third.

Could she deny him that one wish? Maybe it was the thought of making love to her that had kept him going. Maybe he was alive today because of that one desire. It would be heartless to deny him that sustenance, which had brought him back from the brink of death.

There were just so many things to consider. How would they keep it a secret from the other people in the office? How would she let Brendan know without actually telling him? The man was her one true love, but he could be a bit dense when it came to putting the clues together.

Finally, there was her friendship with Matthew to consider. It was as precious to her as her friendship with Darla, maybe more so. And the thought of losing that for a week of meaningless sex didn't seem worth it. Had Matthew considered that? Was he willing to promise her that yes or no he would still be her best friend?

"Matthew, I know you're not really asleep."

He didn't move, but Corinne knew it was only an act. He was probably mentally bracing himself for her answer. Over her sunglasses and beneath the brim of her wide straw hat she took a moment to consider him from a purely sexual standpoint.

There were his shoulders. They were awfully broad. And his face was cut in those severe lines that added intensity to his otherwise placid face. His legs were furred with brown hair and she followed the length of them all the way up to his lap. The man was big. In bed he would probably overwhelm her tiny frame.

What should have frightened her secretly thrilled her. Shaking her head to rid herself of those wicked thoughts, Corinne tried to focus on what was important.

"Matthew, before I give you my answer, I think we need to discuss what will happen to our friendship. I value our relationship. I know it doesn't always seem like that. I've taken you for granted these last few years. After the shooting, though, I realized how important you are to my life. If we were to do this, I would have to be assured that in the end nothing would change between us."

She waited for his reply. After a minute when none came she thought he was taking the sleeping act a little too far. She stood over him, but with his sunglasses on it was difficult to get a read on him one way or other.

"Surely, you are not sleeping at such a critical time as this."

A slight snore passed his lips.

"Ohhh," she huffed. "I pour my heart out to you and you have the nerve to sleep through it."

Another snore.

Searching for the means of retaliation, Corinne spotted it in a yellow sand bucket left abandoned not too far from her camp. Marching over to it, she snatched it up and headed for the ocean. Ankle deep in the cool water, Corinne stooped over and filled the bucket up to its capacity.

Slowly, she made her way back to where Matthew slept, so as not to spill any of her precious revenge. Once she was in position by his head she up-ended the bucket in one fell swoop.

Bolting upright, Matthew shouted, "I'msorryItakeitback forgetIeversaidit." He was drenched, and even in sleep he instinctively knew who the drencher was.

"What were you saying?" she asked sweetly, the bucket dangling from her finger.

"That was my speech for when you tossed the orange juice in my face. A little bit of a delayed reaction." Matthew removed his sunglasses then reached for his towel and dried his face. "So what was this for?"

"You were sleeping," she replied huffily.

"I was tired," he returned.

She tossed the bucket and crossed her arms over her breasts; her eyebrows were raised so high up her head he was afraid they might fall off.

"I was up all night thinking about you. About us," he added and watched the eyebrows descend. Did he know his Rinny or what?

Mollified, she lowered her arms and dropped down on the lounge chair next to him. "I was asking you a very important question."

"Hit me...with the question I mean."

"If we do this." She waved her hands about in front of her as the universal sign for sex and other unmention-ables. "I need to know that when it's over, and it will be over as soon as this trip is over, we'll go back to the way things were. That we'll still be friends."

Matthew plucked one of her hands from the air and held it between his own. "If we do this we'll never go back to the way things were."

Not happy with that answer her shoulders slumped in defeat. "Then I don't think..."

"I'm not done yet. We'll be different because we will have been lovers. There will be an intimacy between us that wasn't there before. But our friendship...that's forged in steel and it is as sturdy as I am."

As sturdy as Matthew. It didn't get much sturdier than that.

"Satisfied?"

"Yes," she answered as she leaned her body into his in a casual gesture. She shouldn't have been surprised to learn that his body was not only big but very firm as well. Yes, they might actually do very well together indeed.

"Does that mean..."

He stuttered a little, Corinne had to believe from the excitement of what lay ahead, but she knew what he was asking regardless. He had reassured her and removed her greatest fear. It would be different and wildly exciting. It would make a profound statement to Brendan when he understood that there were other men in the world who wanted her.

"Yes," she whispered before she could change her mind.

Nodding, Matthew smiled gently. "Good. Now that that's settled, you don't mind if I go back to sleep, do you?" Without another glance at her, he put his sunglasses back and settled down on the lounge chair.

Corinne was beyond offended. She had just told him that she had agreed to make mad passionate love with him and he was going to sleep!

His eyes closed, he added, "I'm going to need all my energy for the night to come." Without peeking, he knew she was considering that information and accepting it as the only valid excuse for wanting to get more sleep.

"Oh. Well, then that's okay," she replied. "You get all the rest you need."

Yep, he definitely knew his Rinny.

5

KNOCK. Knock.

Corinne stared at the door. A glance down at her watch confirmed that the hour was exactly seven as she watched the long hand tick past the number twelve. So here it was. Seven o'clock. The exact moment that he'd promised her he would pick her up for dinner. For dinner then...well...sex.

He wasn't a second late.

Then again why should he be? After all, he was probably as excited as a child on Christmas Eve. He knew what to expect tonight. He knew he was going to have the most exhilarating hours of passion he'd probably ever experienced in his whole life.

Which was something else entirely to consider. Could she live up to his expectations? No doubt he was expecting a lot. After all, she was a Weatherby.

He knocked again. "Rinny?"

She inhaled deeply and exhaled slowly through the tight circle she had formed with her lips. It was an exercise she had learned from her drama coach in high school that was designed to calm her nerves and allowed her to focus on her character. Unfortunately, more often than not she typically ended up hyperventilating. Another good reason why she had chosen finance rather than the stage as a career.

Okay, Corinne, she told herself, *get it together.* Chin up.

Shoulders back. She swung her head forward then whipped it back to give her curls the windblown effect, but instead only managed to make herself dizzy. Striving for balance on her three-inch heels, she teetered to the door.

Desperately, she wanted to gulp, but discovered that her mouth was dryer than a box of salted crackers. Instead she reached for the handle and opened the door.

Matthew, of course, was on the other side of the door. He stood tall in his traditional dark slacks, white shirt and boring tie. He was almost at attention, and he was looking right at her. When Brendan picked her up for their dates, he was always leaning against the door frame or had his back turned to the door.

A protective measure, Corinne rationalized. Brendan felt the need to pretend indifference to protect himself from getting hurt in the end.

Apparently, Matthew had no such fear. Even though he must know that he was going to suffer when it was over and she broke his heart. Part of her couldn't help but admire the courage that took. The blatant honesty of his desire for her stunned her.

Uh-oh, *desire*, wrong choice of words. Corinne could almost taste the crackers in her mouth now.

"Ready?" he queried.

Impulsively, she slammed the door in his face.

HE SUPPOSED that was a no. Matthew stared at the closed door. Belatedly he reached up to touch his nose to make sure it was still there. Thankfully, it was. He knocked on the door again, but only after he took a safety step back.

"Rinny? Is there a problem?"

Have you changed your mind? Do you want to call the whole thing off? Why did you look so scared when you opened the door? The questions that he couldn't ask hung on the tip of his tongue, but he held back. More than likely she was just a little nervous. If she needed a little time to gather herself then he could give her that.

Again the door swung open.

She stood in the frame looking radiant. The pink-flowered sundress she wore should have clashed with her red hair, but instead it only seemed to accentuate all of her colors. The color of her hair, her eyes, her skin. "You sure are pretty," he murmured.

The door slammed closed again.

Matthew was starting to get the impression that he wasn't wanted.

WHY DID he have to be so big, she wondered. Had his shoulders always been that wide? Had his face always been that strong? And the bigger question, when had she become such a frightened little ninny? After all, it was Matthew on the other side of the door. Just Matthew. Her long-time friend and steady companion.

So why was her heart suddenly pounding against her chest? She was pretty sure she'd never felt this way when it was Darla on the other side of the door.

"Rinny, talk to me," he called to her from the other side of the door.

She cracked open the door and saw him through the sliver of space. "I don't think I can do this," she stuttered. Hell, if her heart didn't calm down, she was more than likely going to pass out. Then she really couldn't do it.

"Okay," he said clearly disappointed. "I understand." Matthew smiled a little sadly then turned away from the door.

"Wait! That wasn't your line."

Unfortunately, he hadn't gotten his copy of this particular script. That was okay. No doubt Rinny would fill him in as they went along.

Corinne opened the door a little wider. "What I meant to say was that I thought you might try a little harder before giving up. I mean, really, is it too much to ask for a little effort?"

Matthew sighed. "Rinny, this isn't going to be about me luring you off to bed. It's only going to happen if you want it to. Your problem is that you know you want it to happen, but you're afraid. You also feel a misguided loyalty toward Brendan so you want me to give you some justification for betraying him. But the truth is we're not hurting anybody. We are two single, unattached adults who can do whatever the hell we want. Now are you coming to dinner?"

There was a harshness in his tone that he knew he couldn't hide. He hoped she didn't hear it. He didn't want her to know what it would do to him if she called the whole thing off. After all, they still needed to be friends when this was all over.

It wasn't exactly the speech she was expecting. She was hoping for more of an "I desperately need you, you have to sleep with me, I must have you," sort of monologue. Unfortunately, hers was the only dialogue she could control.

But she did have to admit that he was right. She couldn't help but feel that she was betraying Brendan, although there was no reason for it. Corinne had to get it through her head that until she and Brendan were together, monogamously, they weren't together at all.

Brendan explained the tingle of guilt she felt, but what about the butterflies fluttering around in her belly? And what did Matthew mean when he said she wanted this to happen as much as he did?

He was the seducer in this relationship. She was just the seducee!

The spurt of anger was enough to cure her of her nerves momentarily. "Well there's no point in getting huffy about it. I'll get my bag."

Triumphantly, he smiled as soon as she stepped back into her room. A moment later she stepped out into the hallway with a neon-pink clutch purse in her hand that perfectly matched her dress. Women, he thought, were amazing creatures.

"There's a restaurant down the block that we could walk to. I thought it might be a change from last night."

"Okay," she responded. Because she had little interest in where they were eating, being much more consumed by what was going to happen after dinner than during it, she followed him docilely to the elevators, then out of the hotel lobby and onto the street. All the while scripting possible scenarios in her head. But it was hard to concentrate.

The truth was, now that her anger was over, cooling in the night air as they walked, the butterflies were back. And she knew why. She supposed she should tell him about her revirginization. After all, she'd spent over a year remaking herself into a pure and virtuous woman, saving herself for her one true love.

Unfortunately, that meant she was bound to be a little rusty in the sack.

If she confessed now to being a revirgin, maybe he wouldn't expect so much from her tonight. The idea of disappointing Matthew, in any way, didn't sit well with her. It was bad enough that her reasons for agreeing to this affair were slightly self-serving.

Okay, very self-serving, she admitted to herself. So Matthew deserved at least to get something in return.

Then she laughed inwardly. Who was she kidding? Of course he would be getting something in return. She wasn't going to disappoint him in bed. Maybe it had been a while, but surely sex had to be an awful lot like riding a bike.

Only Corinne had never ridden a bike. As a child she'd preferred dresses to pants and bicycles were not conducive to the wearing of pretty little dresses. What was she going to do?

Corinne stopped in her tracks. Without realizing it she saw that they had already walked the length of the block and were standing outside a small island restaurant offering the finest in native cuisine.

"I don't know about this," she told him.

Somberly, Matthew nodded. "We are taking a big risk."

"It's just that this is all so new," she added.

"New is adventurous."

"New is scary."

"Scary? It's not like you're going to get sick," Matthew said.

She scrunched up her face at him. "I'm not worried about getting sick. I'm worried you'll be disappointed."

He shrugged his shoulders. "I'm pretty easy to please."

"Then I'm worried you'll hate me in the morning when you realize why..."

"As long as they have chicken on the menu..." he said over her.

They stopped speaking. "We're not talking about the same thing, are we?" Matthew asked.

Irritated that she had been baring her soul while he

had been thinking of chicken, Corinne shook her head with short, tight little movements.

"I thought you were nervous about trying the restaurant," he explained lamely.

"I gathered." Corinne stepped inside the restaurant. Like most of the restaurants on the island, the theme was island living. Big colorful flowers filled the room, but since Corinne couldn't smell them she gathered they were fake. The lighting was dim in an effort to create romance, but it was so dark they had a hard time following the hostess to their table. The hostess handed off two menus and left them.

"Yep, chicken on the menu," Matthew announced.

"Goody for you," Corinne quipped.

"Since we both know what I was talking about, why don't you tell me what you were talking about. I don't think I've ever seen you this rattled," he mused. "It's sort of funny."

Her head whipped up in a flash. "Funny?"

Quick, he told himself, *think.* "I just mean that you are usually always so in control. This is a different side to you."

"Well, as long as you're laughing," she said sarcastically.

Matthew reached out to take her hand. He held it until he had her full attention once more. "Talk to me, Rinny. We're friends first, remember?"

Even his hand was big, she thought. It engulfed hers. And strangely it made her feel safe. Had Brendan's touch ever done that? "I don't want to hurt you, Matthew."

"I've got pretty thick skin. It's not bullet-proof, as I've discovered, but I think I can take on one fiery almost-green-eyed almost-redhead."

"I don't want you to hate me," she confided. The guilt was coming back, only this time she didn't feel as if she was betraying Brendan. Rather she felt as if she was betraying Matthew. Betraying him and their friendship.

"Why would I hate you?"

"Because my motives for wanting to do this are selfish. I'm not thinking about you. I'm only thinking about me...and Brendan," she added reluctantly, but truthfully.

It was the last name he wanted to hear tonight. He was honest enough with himself to admit that. But he couldn't be angry. Rinny had made no secret of her feelings, misguided though they may be. The trick was to convince her that those feelings were both misleading and shallow.

He believed that if he could get her into bed, show her physically how much he cared without having to say the words, she would begin to understand the difference between her feelings for Brendan and her feelings for him. What she thought about Brendan was rooted in her fantasies, but what she felt for him was real. He was certain of it.

No, the plan was a good one. Only now he had a condition. "I won't hate you, Rinny."

She sighed in relief.

"But..."

"I think that has to be the most horrible of all the words in the English language," she groaned.

"When this happens, if we both want it to happen, it has got to be because you want me. I'm inviting you to my bed, not you and Brendan. I shudder at the thought."

Since he actually shook his shoulders, Corinne couldn't help but chuckle. "Okay. Deal. If I'm not thinking about you at the critical moment, then we call the whole thing off." She twisted the hand he was currently holding so that they were shaking hands instead of holding them.

"Deal," Matthew agreed. He only hoped their definitions of the "critical moment" were slightly different. He didn't know how capable he would be of calling the whole thing off at that particular point.

Corinne retrieved her hand so she could have something to nervously tangle with the other one. "There is also something you should know. Something I haven't told you yet."

Matthew waited.

"Well, you see, I've always wanted to wait for my true love...but well, then that...and the motorcycle guy...but I read this article...and it's sort of been...and I'm really trying to consider myself...I guess what I'm trying to say is that..."

"Are you a virgin?" Matthew asked astounded.

Naturally, the waiter chose that moment to appear at their table. Corinne could only close her eyes in resigned humiliation and pray that the man would go away.

Delicately, the islander coughed into his hand to clear his throat and to ease the sudden tension at the table. "And what would you both like for dinner this evening?"

They gave their orders and the waiter quickly left, but not before Corinne spotted a definite smile on his face. Turning her focus back to Matthew, she whispered harshly under her breath, "I am not a virgin."

"You're not?"

"No."

"But you said all that stuff about waiting."

"Because I'm a revirgin."

Matthew looked confused. "Can you do that?"

"Yes," she snapped. "And I have. All I was trying to say was that...well, it's been quite some time since I've been with anyone."

"Afraid you're going to be a little rusty in bed?" Matthew asked, an amused smile dancing about his lips. It wasn't like Rinny to admit that she might not be perfect at something.

"Of course not! And will you please keep your voice down!"

He had the good grace to look sheepish. "It's not a surprise, you know."

"It's not?"

"Well, the whole revirgin thing yes, because I'm still not really sure you can do that. But I'm not surprised it has been a while for you."

"And why do you say that?"

"Because I know you and Brendan haven't...you know."

She arched her brow and Matthew instantly interpreted the gesture as a question and answered it. "I heard you two in his office, remember? Brendan said you had unfinished business, and since he only has one kind of business, it didn't take a rocket scientist to determine that you two hadn't done it. Figuring you would be the type to be faithful to him while you were dating it makes sense that it has been a while," he explained.

There should have been outrage. She should have railed against him for eavesdropping on her private conversation. She should have admonished him for asking her in front of the waiter and the surrounding three tables if she was a virgin.

Instead she asked, "And it doesn't...worry you...a little?"

This time Matthew refrained from saying anything as the waiter brought their food. Matthew's chicken arrived, and he greeted it with enthusiasm. Corinne stuck to the salad.

Not that it mattered. The last thing she was capable of doing was choking down a meal when it was conceivable that she might be giving up her revirginity in a few hours. To Matthew and not Brendan. Besides, wasn't there some rule about the number of hours a person had to wait after eating before they had sex? Or was that swimming? She always got the two mixed up.

"Worry, me? Hell no," Matthew assured her in response to her question. Then he wiggled his eyebrows for effect. "I figure I can get you caught up to speed pretty quickly," he said rather confidently while he took another bite of chicken. "And wouldn't you rather have me be the one you decided to lose your revirginity to than Brendan? I can pretty much guarantee you he hasn't been with a revirgin, or virgin for that matter, in a really, really long time."

Corinne speared a cherry tomato with her fork instead of responding to that comment. The answer should have been obvious. Of course she would rather be sharing this night with Brendan. He was, after all, her one true love. He was the one she had waited for. She just wasn't certain of how Brendan might react in that particular situation. Somehow she didn't see him understanding the nature of her sacrifice or why she had done it.

Then again, she'd never claimed that he was perfect, she thought defensively, only that she loved him.

All things considered though, she was glad she would be spending this night with Matthew. There was more to everlasting love than sex. For some people the two never mixed. And there was also more to sex than bodice-ripping passion. For some people that never happened either.

In Corinne's mind sex was also about intimacy. It was about stripping away all the layers that she had applied over the years to make herself desirable and hoping that without them she was still desirable. As long as Matthew was in the room with her, that wasn't a concern. He thought she was beautiful because of who she was, not because of what she was. With him she could be naked, figuratively and literally, and still be safe.

For some unknown reason that thought made her unbearably emotional. For an instant she could feel the tears but she pushed them back. This scene didn't call for tears.

"Are you all right?" Matthew asked, concerned.

Wiping the wetness away from her eyes, Corinne focused on her salad. "I'm fine. You're right, Matthew. I'm glad I'm going to be with you tonight."

He smiled brilliantly and also a little smugly.

"Don't let it go to your head," she commanded sternly.

"Yes, ma'am."

They finished their meals, making idle chitchat along the way. The thought did occur to Matthew that he ought to be making more of an effort to seduce his date. He probably should have been talking about the way her lips compelled him to kiss her, or how he couldn't wait to place baby kisses up and down her smooth and creamy-looking neck. These things were obvious to him, but he knew that women needed the words.

However, from him, he feared they might sound false. He wasn't much for words. Never had been and didn't want to try and start now. Not with Rinny, who knew him better than any woman ever had. She'd see through the words in an instant. Besides, rather than tell her how he felt, he would show her. The first step toward doing that was to get her in his arms.

As they lingered over coffee, Matthew suggested, "You know, that band is playing again at the hotel. I thought maybe we could go dancing first."

Her head tilted, she sighed dramatically and indulgently. It was her patented you-poor-thing expression. "Matthew, I told you last night that you don't need to take me dancing." Corinne hesitated. "At least I think I did. That was before everything started to get really fuzzy."

"But here's the thing. I really can..."

"Besides, I think I would just like to get this whole show on the road," she interrupted. With a determination born of nerves, and the desire to overcome those nerves, Corinne said fatefully, "I'm ready."

When given a choice between dancing and sex, a man will always choose sex. Who was he kidding, given a choice between anything and sex, a man will always choose sex. Sex with Rinny broke the scale altogether.

"Okay," he replied and had to chuckle at himself as his own nerves took over. This was it. This was his chance. He had this night. If everything went well, he also had the length of their vacation together to show her that his love was real. That he was the real thing for her. Solid. Enduring. Loyal. All the things that Golden Boy wasn't.

Actually, it put a new twist on the whole act. There was meaning to it now. There would be a powerful emotion behind every kiss, each touch. Matthew dug back into his memory and tried to recall what it had felt like to make love to Debbie.

There had definitely been emotion, but there had always been distance as well. Looking back on it, Matthew supposed he had been responsible for that. Partly because he knew she didn't care much for the act, and partly because it had always been in his nature to hold back. He didn't trust people easily. He supposed there should be some childhood traumatic event that he could blame for that although he didn't remember anything in particular. It was just who he was. He liked to keep to himself even when he was with people.

Except when he was around Rinny. She was different. She made him a different man. All because he trusted her. He couldn't answer, "why her?" He only knew that, with her, he held nothing back.

But that wasn't completely true, he realized. He'd never told her the truth about what he felt for her. He didn't think he needed to. He'd always assumed that his feelings were obvious, but Rinny never seemed to see beyond his friendship.

He couldn't blame her for that though. Just because he had recognized something inside her instantly, because something had told him that this was the girl for him and that everything was going to work out all right in the end didn't mean she had felt the same connection. And because she never saw beyond the facade of friendship, he might have gone on, content to be her friend only.

If he hadn't gotten shot.

When he had wakened from his coma and the first thing he'd seen was her face, that voice inside him, the one he'd tried to ignore had begun to shout. It screamed: *Her.*

And that had been the very first thought that had surfaced through the haze of drugs. Followed by an intense desire for a glass of water—he'd been really thirsty. But

it was the memory of that shouted whisper and the realization that the end might have come a lot sooner than
he would have liked that had finally compelled him to
act.

And here he was about to make love with Rinny for
the very first time.

Standing, Matthew threw more than enough money
down on the table to pay the check, and reached for her
hand. Corinne stood and linked her hand with his. Their
fingers entwined. He could almost hear the click. The fit.
The skin against skin that didn't rub against each other
so much as it meshed together.

Corinne smiled. "Let's go."

The night had grown slightly cooler since they had
first entered the restaurant, but the overall condition
was still balmy. Automatically, Corinne reached up to
test the condition of her curls. It was as she suspected:
frizzville. Desperately she tried to smooth down what
she could, as inconspicuously as possible, but knew the
task was futile.

He must have sensed what she was doing because
suddenly he stopped in his tracks and turned so that he
was facing her. "Corinne, I don't care what your hair
looks like."

"I don't know what you're talking about," she said
haughtily. Caught in the act of sprucing, but not willing
to admit it, Corinne attempted to lower her hand from
her head only to discover that she had gotten her fingers
caught in her own curls.

"Help," she squeaked. Matthew tried to help pull her
hand free, but only managed to pull her hair instead.
"Ow!"

"Hold still," he returned. Finally, her hand was free.
Her hair, however, was a mess.

Matthew said nothing. Instead he simply chuckled, then cupped her face in his large hands and lowered his lips to hers.

The surprise mixed with the power of his kiss was enough to weaken Corinne's knees. It was like no other kiss she had ever experienced. He didn't just kiss her. He stole her lips. He made them his. He offered no quarter. His tongue pushed past her teeth and his taste invaded her. Colors swam before her eyes and she had to clutch his shoulders to keep from sinking to the ground.

After what felt like forever, Matthew backed off. She heard her own moan of disappointment and couldn't believe that it was her actually making that sound. Not only that, but she was forced to reach out to him just until she could once again find her balance.

"What was that for?" she asked as she tested her lips with her tongue to see if they were still attached to her face. They were. A bit swollen, but there.

"Because I wanted to. Because I know you were thinking that your hair is getting frizzy and that somehow that might make you less attractive. I wanted to prove to you that wasn't true."

She nodded.

He took her hand again and they resumed their walk back to the hotel.

Finally she asked, "So you think my hair is frizzy?"

Loudly, he groaned.

The two entered the hotel and stepped up to the elevator. With a casualness he wasn't feeling, Matthew asked, "My place or yours?" He smiled. "I always wanted to say that."

There was a choice? Of course there was a choice. It was a simple choice. Not really anything to get upset over. But her system was already on overload with the choice she had made to sleep with him. Now he was asking her to make another choice and she couldn't do it.

There were all these factors. All her stuff was in her room. But then again, what if Brendan called and Matthew answered the phone. However, that might not be a bad thing. Except then Matthew would see all the dresses she had tried on getting ready for this night and would think that she went to a lot of effort to please him. Which of course she had, but a man should never know the amount of effort a woman puts into any one given date.

Oh, she was fast becoming flustered. But he was standing there waiting for her to say something. Anything.

"Yours. No, mine. No, yours. No, mine."

Patiently, he waited. He figured there would be a few more rounds of this before she actually decided.

"Definitely yours. But on second thought, I think mine. Yes, mine. Not that yours wouldn't be okay. I'm sure it's fine. Okay, then we'll go to yours. Yes, here we are going to yours. Decision made."

They got on the elevator with Corinne standing closest to the floor buttons. Immediately, she hit her floor. "Mine."

"Yours," Matthew said simultaneously. As nervous as she was, being on her home turf might take the edge off her unreasonable fear.

The doors slid open and Corinne burst out of the gate like a stallion on its way to the finish line. Key in hand, she reached her door and opened it. "You have to wait here for a second. I need to…tidy up." She threw open the door and slammed it in his face for the third time that evening.

Matthew was starting to get a complex.

The room was a disaster. Dresses, skirts, shorts, practically every item of clothing that she had brought was strewn about the room. It would take her more than an hour to refold everything and put it back in its place. As patient as Matthew was, Corinne didn't think he would wait an hour.

And she was ready. Really ready to get this show on the road. She had waited twenty-seven years for this night....

According to the article she had read, it was best to forget all previous experiences. So for tonight she decided she would pretend that this was her first time. A night she had fantasized about. Dreamt about. Longed for.

Of course in reality Danny Hatch had smooth-talked his way into the back seat of her mother's Mercedes after three wine coolers and a promise that he'd take her to the prom. Fifteen minutes after that, the deed was done. That night hadn't quite lived up to her fantasies. And, honestly, neither had any encounters since.

She was hoping Matthew could do better.

Scooping up the expensive and delicate fabrics, she sprinted to the nearest closet, opened it, and let the clothes fall where they may. On top of them she threw shoe after shoe, a few scarves, her various handbags, a straw hat, and an assortment of accessories. With a little effort she pushed the door shut. Quickly, she made her way to the bathroom where she found her perfume bottle on the vanity. A few spritzes about her throat and around her ankles and she was ready. A silent prayer to the goddess of love that she hadn't lost her touch after her period of inactivity, and her pre-sexual preparations were complete.

Chin high, she marched to the door and threw it open. "I'm ready," she announced breathlessly.

A scent of perfume wafted to the vicinity of his nose. Matthew was reminded of one of those cartoon images where the scent turns into the hand, a finger crooks and the silly character is lured into certain danger. He supposed he was the silly character in his own metaphor, but he didn't think he was being lured into danger.

He stepped into a neat room. He had heard her running about so he assumed that she had performed a miraculous cleanup. It didn't matter. The only thing in the room he had eyes for was Rinny. She filled his senses. He moved toward her and reached to cup her face in his palm.

The uncertainty was there in her eyes, in the way her lips quivered ever so slightly, but accompanying it was expectation. He hoped he didn't disappoint her. He lowered his lips to hers and touched their fullness briefly. Then he felt her hands on his chest, which would have been okay if she wasn't pushing him away.

"Wait," she shouted.

Reining in his passion, Matthew straightened, preparing for another speech on why she couldn't do this. Perhaps he had pushed her into this too soon. Perhaps he should have given the island atmosphere and their natural connection more time to work their magic.

"My contacts," she announced. "I should take them out first."

Suppressing a sigh of relief, he nodded.

She trotted off to the bathroom and returned a hazel-eyed girl. "You don't mind, right?"

"Of course not," he told her. "I think your eyes are beautiful just the way they are."

Disregarding his compliment she returned to her position, snug up against his chest. Hesitantly she put her hands on his waist. "Okay, where were we?"

Sliding his fingers through her hair and nipping a bit at her lips, Matthew reminded her, "We were right about here."

Again he kissed her, and this one was no less potent than the others had been. It was almost like an electrical shock to her system. An evil whisper of an idea snaked its way through her mind. This kiss wasn't like any she had ever experienced. This kiss, his kiss, was more powerful than Brendan's.

No! Corinne denied the thought before it could take root. She was in love with Brendan. She had been in love with him for months and months. It was true love. Deep unending love. Not the flighty emotion her family practiced on a regular basis. The kind of love that made the fairy tales. So the most passionate kiss she had ever felt had to belong to Brendan.

What she shared with Matthew was friendship. Trust. Comfort.

Her knees buckled when she felt his hand cup her breast. "Oh my," she breathed.

Matthew, on the other hand, was a little confused. He believed he was touching her breast. That had been his intent when he had slid his hand down her neck, over her throat and chest. But what he held in his hand felt more like a pillow. Slipping his hands behind her back, Matthew found the zipper to the sundress and pulled it down. Instantly the off-the-shoulder sleeves lost their grip and fell down her arms revealing a strapless bra that not only supported her breasts, but also seemed to increase their lushness.

Realizing that he was looking at her, Corinne gazed down at herself. "Push-up bra," she explained as he poked his finger at the cushioned cup. "Amazing invention."

Matthew's hands left the zipper and slid back up her back. With deft fingers he removed the lingerie and let it fall to the floor between them.

Two pert breasts greeted him and he felt a punch of lust hit him low and hard in the gut. "You're perfect." He sighed, as he cupped her naked breast in his hand. "Utterly perfect."

"You don't think I'm too small?"

Since he was too overcome with passion to clearly form words, Matthew did the next best thing and lowered his mouth to the tip of her breast. He sucked the morsel in his mouth until he heard her cry out. He tried to back off, knowing that they had all night and not wanting to rush to any conclusions. But when he stepped back to gain a little control, she followed and leaned her soft body against him.

It was too much. Waiting was no longer an option. Offering a silent apology because he imagined that this first time was going to be a little rushed, he promised himself that he would make it up to her the second time around. It's just that the way things were now, he was feeling so urgent he didn't know if he'd have the willpower he needed to take it slowly.

"Rinny, I can't wait."

Shifting positions, he scooped her off the floor, leaving her dress and bra behind. He carried her to the bed and laid her out before him.

The sight of her stretched out on the bed in nothing more than a pair of panties and high-heeled sandals was almost more than he could take. She was perfect. A fantasy come to life. She was making him so hot that he could feel the beads of sweat popping out on his head

and his hands were trembling. Then she stirred rest-
lessly on the bed and he felt another punch to his gut.

Only this time it was stronger. And really, it felt less
like passion and more like...

"I think I'm going to be sick!"

6

"LET'S EVALUATE," Corinne said aloud to the empty room.

She was practically naked. Her very soul was exposed and vulnerable. Her knees were weak with passion and her belly was queasy in such a delicious way that she had wanted that feeling to go on all night. And since she had read enough women's magazines to thoroughly understand the concept, if not the practice, of the female orgasm, she was reasonably sure that she had been on the right track. That was, until the man who was making love to her had rushed to the bathroom to toss his cookies.

The natural and normal thing to do would have been to break down into tears. Maybe run sobbing from the room to the beach or some such place where she could suffer her humiliation in private. It was definitely a consideration. If any scene called for tears this one most assuredly did.

But in the end there was only one thing to do.

Corinne rolled off the bed and scooped up her dress. She threw it over her head and followed her friend into the bathroom to return the favor he had offered her that very morning.

After a time, when his stomach had eased its spasms, the two sat back against the tub in the quiet coolness of the bathroom.

"It must have been the chicken," he uttered weakly.

It hadn't been her intention to laugh, but she couldn't help it. Not that Matthew's pain was something to chuckle about. But the fact that they seemed to get nauseous when they started kissing each other *was* rather amusing.

"I don't know, Matthew. Maybe we have the wrong kind of chemistry. It seems that any time our mouths come into contact something bad happens. Who knows what might happen if we actually have sex? It could kill us," she said, still laughing.

Matthew tried for a weak smile, but he didn't have it in him. He had just ruined the most important night of his life all because he wanted to show Rinny that he could be adventurous enough to try an island restaurant. Damn, why couldn't he have gone with the steak! "I should go down to that restaurant and give the chef a piece of my mind."

He started to stand, but Corinne could see the tremor in his limbs. "I have a better idea. Why don't you use my toothbrush and get comfortable. I'll tuck you in myself."

She left him to his privacy and closed the door behind him.

Tuck him in? There were possibilities in that scenario. Then his stomach rolled, and Matthew instinctively knew that if she did tuck him into bed, all he could hope to do would be to sleep it off. Viciously, he yanked his tie from around his neck and unbuttoned his shirt. It would have been right about now that Corinne would have been undressing him. She would have unbuttoned each button on his shirt. Slowly, he was sure, until it drove him mad. Then she would have reached for his pants.

Matthew groaned silently as his stomach rolled once more. His misery was truly profound. He washed up and tossed his shirt, undershirt, slacks, socks and tie over the shower railing so as not to wrinkle them unnecessarily and was about to step out of the bathroom in nothing more than a pair of boxers. Then he remembered his scar.

He glanced down at his chest and saw the mark that reminded him daily that life was precious. It's not as though she wouldn't see it eventually, but now probably wasn't the best time. He'd prefer to have her so dazed by passion that it would barely register when she first saw it. He grabbed his undershirt and put it back on, then stepped out into the bedroom.

Corinne had already tucked herself into bed. Above the covers he could see that she wore a white gown with short puffy sleeves and a pink bow at the neck.

Part little girl. Part seductress.

Sporting a pair of thick glasses, she had her nose hidden behind the cover of a paperback novel. Matthew now understood why she had gone for the contacts. The glasses looked like pop-bottle bottoms and practically covered her whole face. Of course he didn't necessarily understand why the contacts had to be green, but that was his Rinny. Always taking that extra step.

Sensing his presence, she looked up at him and smiled. With one hand she pulled back the comforter on the bed and patted it.

"Come on. You'll sleep here tonight so I can keep my eye on you and make sure you don't need to be taken to the hospital."

He should have been overjoyed. He was going to sleep in Rinny's bed after all. But somehow this wasn't how he had pictured it. Disappointed, frustrated and still slightly nauseous, Matthew accepted the generous invitation and filled the space on the side of the bed that she had left vacant.

Once he was on his back his stomach began to ease, but he could feel a heavy lethargy overtake his muscles and knew that sleep wasn't far off. Rinny plumped the pillow behind him to make him more comfortable. The action reminded him of his childhood days when his mother would do the same.

"Why didn't you toss me out on my ear, Rinny?"

"For the same reason you didn't run from my room earlier this morning. I care about you."

"This was supposed to be our big night." He sighed.

Hesitantly, she stuttered, "Well...it's...I mean...it's not like our vacation is over. There's still time."

He supposed he should take some comfort in the fact that she hadn't totally given up on him. "You know, Rinny, you don't need those push-up bras. Your breasts are beautiful just the way they are."

He heard the swoosh of the pillow before it actually hit his face. He imagined her own face was currently a pretty shade of pink right now and her eyes were probably sparkling with annoyance behind her super-thick glasses.

"Don't you worry about my undergarments. Now go to sleep," she ordered.

She pulled the pillow away, and he was able to take in her expression. It was just as he had imagined. She was so precious to him in that moment that his heart practically hurt.

"When I was a boy and I got sick and my mother tucked me in and plumped my pillow, she would finish by telling me a story," he mentioned casually.

"She would, huh?"

"And since I happen to know about your career on the side, I thought maybe you could..."

"Say no more," Corinne interrupted. Nobody ever had to twist her arm to get her to tell a story. She placed the book on the nightstand along with her glasses and turned out the lights. "Once upon a time," she began, "there was a beautiful redheaded, green-eyed princess...."

"Sable-haired princess with red highlights and hazel eyes," Matthew corrected her.

"Who's telling this story?" she asked sternly.

"You are," he mumbled.

"Very well then. Anyway, this princess lived in a huge castle with servants and all the luxuries she could ever want, but she wasn't happy."

"Why not?"

"Because she didn't have the one thing that she thought mattered most in the world: love. She searched the kingdom high and low for this love but could not find that one magical person who would touch her heart and complete her.

"Her parents, the king and queen, brought before her prince after prince to chose from, but the princess knew that the princes were only after the throne and her wealth. They didn't want her. So she decided the only way for anyone to love her just for herself was to shuck her princess garb..."

"Now we're cooking," Matthew interjected sleepily.

"...and replace it with peasant garb."

"Oh. Boring."

Offended, Corinne pounded her fists against the pillow in a huff. "Boring? What am I supposed to do, have the princess walking around the kingdom buck-naked?

This is not some twisted version of 'The Emperor's New Clothes.'"

"That sounds promising. Could you do that one next?"

"No! Now, no more comments from the peanut gallery."

"Yes, ma'am," Matthew humbly agreed and was grateful she couldn't see his grin in the dark.

"So anyway, there was our princess decked out like a peasant and this prince came riding into town. He had come to woo the princess, but he took one look at the peasant girl and was instantly struck by her beauty. He decided he must have her despite her low station, and he got down on his knee and proposed to her right there in the dirt and mud."

"What if it was a trick?"

"Excuse me?" she questioned, her tone as imperious as he imagined her fictional princess's might be.

"What if this so-called prince knew she was hiding in peasant garb all along and just pretended that he had fallen in love with her? What sort of man is this prince anyway?"

Corinne huffed. Leave it to Matthew to ruin a perfectly good story with practical questions. "It wasn't a trick. And he's a fine man and they lived happily ever after! Except for this one pesky friend that the princess had who kept trying to break them up. But in the end he recognized true love when he saw it and he was glad that his friend had found such happiness with the man she loved. Then the princess's best friend and her new husband became best friends as well and all three of them lived happily ever after...after."

"Now that *is* a fairy tale," Matthew quipped.

"Go to sleep, Matthew."

"Yes, ma'am," he replied and let his heavy eyes close.

Corinne, however, had no such luck. She tossed. She turned. She listened to Matthew breathing steadily, slowly throughout the night. And she contemplated the burning question that kept replaying in her mind.

Why did it feel so right to have Matthew in bed beside her?

MORNING, for some inexplicable reason, came earlier on islands. Corinne's theory was that it was the water and sand doing a better job of reflecting the sunlight into an unsuspecting sleeper's room, thus waking her before her time. She wasn't sure of the exact scientific nature of the whole thing, but she did know that 7:00 a.m. was way too early for her to be considering opening her eyes. Especially on her vacation.

But the blasted sun wouldn't give up. And as tightly as she shut her eyes, the feeling that something was amiss on this particular morning wouldn't let her go.

"Let's evaluate," she grumbled. "I'm in my hotel bed. I am not hungover like I was yesterday. A major bonus. I was going to sleep with Matthew last night, but instead…"

Matthew. He was in the bed with her. It all came crashing back. So that explained the heavy weight that was pressing against her back. She felt as though she was being hugged by a bear. Or at least a very large man, which made sense since she was being hugged by a very large man. Matthew had one arm slung over her waist, with his hand pressed against her belly, which was pressing her back against his chest and flat stomach and…

Oh my.

So it is true what they say about what happens to

some men in the morning. Corinne couldn't remember the last time she'd woken up in a man's arms, so her memory was a little hazy on the subject. The appropriate thing would have been to slip out of his embrace and create some distance between them. Sure, they had planned to make love last night, but maybe Matthew's getting sick was divine intervention. Perhaps this was fate's way of telling her that she should be true to her heart. And her heart wanted Brendan.

Right, heart?

No, *want* was the wrong word, she thought before her heart could actually answer. Her heart had chosen Brendan. And the heart can only choose once. At least *her* heart. The fickle gene didn't run through her the way it did for the rest of her family. She was sure of it.

So why wasn't she moving? Matthew shifted in his sleep, his arm around her waist instinctively tightening his hold. Then his lips started nuzzling her neck. Okay, this was an interesting position. In fact it was quite comfortable. Perhaps she was being a little hasty with her decision to get out of bed. Waking up with a man was something she should get used to. After all, someday she would share a bed every night with Matthew...Brendan. Brendan.

Pleased with her decision to remain, Corinne allowed herself to snuggle more deeply into his embrace. Her bottom was now in direct contact with his morning arousal. Not for the first time she wondered at the strangeness of the male body, so different from her own. And Matthew, if her bottom was any judge, was manlier...than any vague memory she had. Certainly more manly than Carlos. His only truly impressive feature had been his hair.

Struck by a burst of curiosity, Corinne decided she

wanted to see exactly what she was letting herself in for...so to speak. It was, she decided, her right as a woman contemplating sex with the man in question.

Another decision made, Corinne began to turn into Matthew's embrace, slowly shifting her weight from her right side onto her back then turning onto her left side. Her lips at this point were practically in contact with his neck. And when she inhaled, she breathed in a unique male scent that was inherently Matthew.

Wow.

He smelled really good. Potent. Masculine. So different from her own softly perfumed scent. It set off tiny little bells over all her body and made goose bumps rise on her skin. And she thought that at least one issue had been settled for her during this trip.

She hadn't stopped sleeping with other men because of any kind of distaste for sex. There had been times when it had been so easy not to accept an obvious offer from a date, or even from Brendan for that matter, that Corinne had begun to worry about her libido. But if the gooey feeling in her stomach, and the tightness she felt in her nipples, and the little rippling of tension in her thighs were any indication, her sex drive was alive and well.

No, she definitely hadn't made her commitment to renewed chastity because she was sexually frigid. So why had it been so easy for her to turn Brendan down?

That thought didn't have time to take root. Matthew shifted again, brought on by her change in position no doubt, but continued to sleep, if his near-silent snoring was any indication. His mouth was parted ever so slightly. Corinne was struck by a sudden urge to thrust her tongue inside his mouth and watch his eyes open with shock and desire.

But first things were first. She had come for a peek of his Willie, or Johnson, or little friend or whatever silly little pet name he had chosen for the essence of his manhood. Men could be so ridiculous sometimes.

Creating a few inches of space between their bodies, Corinne let her hand trail southbound over his undershirt until it reached elasticity.

No movement from the subject.

Target in reach. All systems on go.

Now for the critical step: penetration.

Ever so gently Corinne pushed her finger inside the elastic band of the boxers that hugged Matthew's waist so snugly. The material gave and before she realized what was happening her hand was inside his boxers, the back of her knuckles brushing against the rough hair of his belly and groin.

Penetration complete.

Closing her hand around the crinkled band, Corinne pulled until there was at least an inch between the boxers and Matthew's body. Distance achieved. All she had to do was duck her head and take a peek.

Slowly, shyly, she lowered her eyes like a boy about to look at his first girlie magazine, partly fascinated, partly nervous, and so turned on she felt as if she was about to burst. Just a little lower and...

"What are you doing?"

"Ahh!!!" she screamed. The power of her shriek sent her sprawling backward until she rolled off the bed and onto the floor with a loud thunk.

Wincing in pain, her head having hit the nightstand on the way down, Corinne squinted at Matthew, who was staring down at her. "Didn't your mother ever tell you not to startle people like that?" she scolded.

"Didn't your mother ever tell you not to peek into a

boy's shorts? You never know what you're going to find down there." His grin was infectious.

She couldn't help but smile herself. Still she needed to retain some self-respect. "I was...I was..."

"Oh, I can't wait to hear this excuse," Matthew said.

Her hands waved about. She hemmed. She hawed. And for the first time since he'd met the infamous Corinne Weatherby, she was at a loss for words. He was about to bail her out and let her know that if anything he'd been flattered by her curiosity when suddenly she screeched, "Ah-ha!"

"Ah-ha, what?"

"I saw a snake," she stated, her face stone-sober. "You know the islands are full of them."

"A snake?"

"Yep. A big one."

Awkwardly, he blushed, "Well, thanks..."

"Poisonous, too," she continued. "I was just trying to extract it before it bit you."

Matthew couldn't help but cringe at the mental image she evoked.

"Fortunately for both of us, I think it's slithered away."

"If it hadn't at your screech, it certainly did at the whole biting comment," Matthew mumbled grumpily.

Corinne sat up, a more serious thought interrupting their morning reverie. "How are you feeling?"

"Fine," he stated. "It was just a bout of food poisoning. Nothing serious. Maybe the snake bit the chicken I ate last night."

"Maybe," she murmured. But somehow she doubted it. "So what now?"

"It's a beautiful morning. Would it be lazy of us to

spend another day together on the beach?" Matthew
suggested.

It wasn't the first idea that came to his mind, but he
knew something about Corinne this morning that he
hadn't known before last night. She wanted him. He'd
felt it when he'd kissed her last night. Pure desire, just
for him. Now some of that feeling could be attributed to
sickness, but not all of it. He was sure of it.

And there was the fact that she had tried to get into his
shorts. Literally. For the first time Matthew felt as if he
might be gaining the upper hand in this relationship.
Maybe, just maybe, a little anticipation of what was to
come might open her eyes further to the truth about her
feelings for him.

"Vacations are about being lazy. But how do you
want to start off the day?" Corinne asked, using her
most sultry tones. She crawled back onto the bed like a
cat on the prowl, trying not to wince at the throbbing
pain in her head and instead look seductive.

It hadn't been her intention to make love to Matthew
for the first time in broad daylight. After all, a girl liked
to keep a few of her secrets hidden in the dark that first
time. However, Matthew had proven to her time and
time again that she didn't have to worry about her appearance with him. He was happy with her the way she
was.

Which was a good thing because she had a little mole
by her belly button, and if all things went as planned, he
was going to get an up-close-and-personal view of it.
Corinne started to reach for him to run her hand along
his chest, but as soon as she did, Matthew exited the bed.

"The best place to start is breakfast. I have to go back
to my room to change, so how about we meet downstairs in half an hour?"

Her expression of utter confusion was priceless. Then,

after the confusion, came downright sulkiness, and Matthew knew he would carry that face with him for the rest of his days. He all but skipped to the bathroom to collect his things. He stepped into his pants and tossed his shirt on, but left the tie swinging around his neck and the buttons of his shirt unbuttoned.

When he returned to the bedroom he found Corinne draped across the bed, her tiny frame as long as she could make it. One hand rested on her curved hip, her other hand was holding her head up, and her eyes were closed to slits. She looked like something out of a Mae West movie. And he did want to come up and see her sometime, but presently it was more fun to make her squirm.

"Are you sure you're hungry?" she asked in a throaty voice reminiscent of her mother's.

Oh boy, was he hungry. Soon, he promised himself. If he gave her a day to think about it, and work herself up to it, come tonight she'd be ripping the clothes off his back.

"Yep, I'm starved. So you won't mind if I beat you downstairs by a few minutes, will you? Got to go. See you soon." He bolted out of the room and slammed the door behind him a bit too forcefully, but he knew if he stayed another minute all his planning would have been for naught.

Realizing he had made good on his escape, and knowing his Rinny like he did, Matthew figured her pride would be pretty piqued right about now. No doubt she would spend the day attempting to lure him in an assembly of ways that she was scripting in her head this very minute.

He couldn't wait.

"Humph." She sighed as her fist made contact with the pillow. This was not how this morning was supposed to go. Of course, last night hadn't gone as planned either, but this morning was supposed to be different. In the scene she had directed in her mind, somewhere between the salad and the walk back to the hotel, there had been a lot more snuggling and kissing. And a lot more of the tingling feelings that Matthew had elicited with just a simple touch.

Instead, he was gone, she didn't get the preview she'd been hoping for, and to top it off she was probably going to have a bruise on her bottom from where she hit the floor.

Corinne sat up in the bed. Maybe the problem was her. Maybe she wasn't sexy enough. She certainly wasn't her sister. She wasn't even her mother when it came to that department. And it had been some time since she'd actually worked to entice a man into bed.

The phone on the table next to the bed rang and startled her out of her thoughts.

She smiled smugly. Perhaps Matthew had reconsidered exactly what he wanted for breakfast. Coughing a bit to clear her throat, she picked up the phone. "Hello," she whispered huskily.

"Corinne? Is that you?"

"Darla?" Corinne asked, recognizing her friend's voice.

"Hi. What's the matter with your voice? Hey, you didn't get sick on vacation, did you? That would really stink."

"No, I'm not sick," Corinne said in her normal voice as she tried not to be disappointed that it wasn't Matthew on the other end of the phone. "What are you calling for? Is something wrong?"

"Not wrong. But the office is buzzing. It seems that Matthew requested vacation time right after you left and then the next day he up and disappeared. Everybody is wondering where he went."

"You know where he is," Corinne told her friend, knowing now why she had called. "You told him where to find me."

"You mean he did it. He actually followed you down there. I hoped he would, but I didn't know if he had it in him. Go Matthew!"

Corinne frowned into the phone. "I can't believe my best friend is rooting against me. You know how I feel about Brendan."

"I know, but I can't help it. I like Matthew for you better. So how is it going?"

"It's going," Corinne said cryptically. Then, deciding she had a golden opportunity to get advice from a friend, she confided, "You know how I told you that I've been, well, out of commission for some time?"

"Uh-oh. Did you forget how to do it?"

"No!" Corinne exclaimed. "It's just that…let's just say that my seduction techniques are a little rusty."

"I see. You know what you need?"

"What?"

"A refresher course."

"It's not like they offer that as an activity down here," Corinne said sarcastically. "Tennis lessons sure, but I haven't found one class on how to seduce a man."

"No, silly, I meant you need help from a pro. And you've got one of the best right in your own family."

That was true. If anyone could give her lessons on how to seduce a man it was her mother.

"You think I should call her?"

"I think you should," Darla stated definitively. "Now,

I have to go. This call is costing me a fortune and I don't want to blow the pot I just won."

"Pot? Won? Darla did you bet on whether or not Matthew would follow me down here?"

"Not exactly. There was a little more to it than that."

"Darla!"

"Got to go! Love you." With that the phone disconnected.

Corinne glared at the receiver in her hand hoping that her friend could feel her fury from so many miles away. *A little more to it than that.* Corinne didn't have to struggle to guess exactly what that meant. When she got back, she would plan a suitable revenge for her very good friend. But right now she had more pressing problems. And Darla had given her some good advice.

Reaching over to grab the phone from the table, Corinne punched in the necessary numbers for an outside line. A few seconds later, many miles away, a phone rang. And rang. And rang.

"Hello," her mother's voice whispered over the lines.

"Mother? Is that you?" If it was possible, her mother's voice was even huskier than normal.

"Corinne? Do you know what damn time it is?"

Oops. "I'm guessing about five in the morning your time."

"It's earlier than I damn well thought," Grace cursed. "Is something wrong, honey? Are you all right?"

"Yes," Corinne began. "But..."

"Then why are you damn well calling me at such an ungodly damn hour?"

So much for motherly concern. Corinne figured it was best to get to the point. "I need to know how to seduce a man. And Myra is on location."

"Myra!" her mother shouted, perked up by the nature

of the topic. "Your sister doesn't know half of what I know about seducing a damn man. She's so beautiful she's never had to work at it much. Now you are another damn story. You are going to need all the tricks I can teach you over this damn phone."

Corinne was sure that her mother didn't mean that to be as insulting as Corinne took it. "Okay, Mother. I'm listening."

"Step damn one..."

SHE WAS LATE, but that wasn't a surprise. Corinne was always late. Still, Matthew began to worry. He had been pretty sure that his retreat strategy was the right one an hour ago, but now he wasn't so sure. What if he'd left her and she'd done something unpredictable like start crying. Matthew figured his Rinny had enough self confidence to know that he wasn't rejecting her, merely prolonging the foreplay, but she'd admitted that it had been a while since her last physical relationship.

It was conceivable that in the area of intimacy she was more vulnerable than she was in other areas of her life. He should go find her and make love to her just so that she would know that he desired her as he had no other woman he'd ever known. And if he got a little something out of it, too, well a man had to do what a man had to do.

Good plan, he told himself.

As he was about to stand, he spotted Rinny coming toward him across the dining room. She was in a tropical-print one-piece bathing suit with a matching sarong and high-heeled sandals that did everything they could to draw attention to her legs. She carried a floppy straw hat large enough to block out the sun for the whole island and a matching straw bag over her shoulder. Her hair was tossed about as if she had just rolled out of bed, but Matthew knew it took several brands of hair gel and mousse to achieve the look. He knew because he'd seen all the cans and sprays in her bathroom that morning.

Boy, she was pretty. Even without mousse.

"Am I late?" Of course she was. That had been her mother's first rule. Always make the man wait. It builds the anticipation. The benefit of this particular strategy was that Corinne was already a natural at being late. She simply needed more time than most to prep, but it was helpful to know that it was also useful as a seduction tactic.

"No," he lied indulgently. He gazed deeply into her fake green eyes, but found no redness or puffiness. Apparently, she hadn't been crying, which tossed his idea about her vulnerability out the window. Oh well. "Breakfast?"

"That's okay, I'll pass. Got to watch the figure." And so saying she placed a hand on her sarong-covered hip and patted it slightly.

Matthew envied that hand. "Let's hit the beach then."

He stood and tossed his napkin on top of his plate and they were off. Corinne walked with him for a while, then tucked her arm inside the crook of his elbow.

"You don't mind?" she queried, her gaze falling to where their arms were linked.

"Not at all." In fact, he rather liked being linked to Rinny. He saw their entwined arms as sort of symbolic.

The beach was reasonably crowded, but Matthew and Corinne were able to stake out their own camp. Matthew sat first on the lounge chair.

As surreptitiously as she could manage, Corinne pushed her lounge chair slightly closer to his with her shin. Unfortunately, the beach chairs weren't the lightest pieces of furniture she had ever encountered. It took several grunts, a few kicks and what she knew would amount to another ugly bruise before the chairs were close enough for her satisfaction. Luckily, Matthew had been staring out to sea the whole time.

What was she doing with that lounge chair? he wondered. As well as he knew his Rinny there were still times when she left him guessing. She plunked herself into the lounge chair, her arm touching his, and sighed. She pulled the hat on and shade instantly covered her upper body.

"What a view. The water is so blue it almost hurts my eyes," she murmured. As she did she touched his forearm several times to make her point.

It had to be part of some strategy, Matthew guessed. Rinny normally touched people when she spoke, when she wasn't busy waving her hands about in front of her face, but even this was a little much for her. Just as he'd predicted, he thought smugly. She was trying to seduce him. It was going to be a glorious day. And the night... well, that went without saying.

"Yeah," he returned, trying to make conversation and keep his thoughts focused on the present rather than on her luscious naked body rolling beneath him. "I almost can't wait to go home and try to see if I can duplicate it with my paints."

"You paint?" Corinne asked, shocked that she didn't know that about him and more shocked that he actually painted. Matthew was a numbers man. A CPA. The bottom line. The end result. The net profit and loss. He wasn't the type to paint.

Then again he didn't seem to be the type that could kiss a girl's socks off and make her so slack-kneed she could barely stand, but he did that, too. "What do you paint?"

"I..."

"What medium do you use?"

"Well..."

"Oils? Watercolors?"

"Actually..."

"Can I see your work?" Corinne asked, continuing her barrage of questions. "And most important...have you ever painted me?"

Matthew thought about the canvas that he had hanging in his bedroom. To the untrained eye it was a red splotch with what could have passed as eyes and a nose. To him it was his Rinny. Still, he didn't think he would share that piece of information. She would want to see it and somehow he guessed that Rinny wouldn't appreciate his abstract representation of her.

"I'm not very good," he finally got in. "I just do it as a break from the numbers. It keeps the other half of my brain working. You're lucky. You're talented with both sides of your brain."

"I am? But I don't paint."

"No, I meant your acting. You're a great financial controller and you're a great actress."

"I don't act," she said stiffly. She wasn't a great actress. That was why she could never follow in her family's very large footsteps. She didn't have her mother's or her sister's looks. And she didn't have her father's or her brother's talent.

"Sure you act. Every time you tell a story you become the characters involved. It's why the kids are so fascinated by you."

She flipped her wrist in the air in dismissal. "That's not acting, that's just..."

"Acting," he finished. "In front of the most challenging audience a performer can face. I've never seen you lose a crowd's attention yet."

That made Corinne think. "How many times have you visited story time at the library?"

Every time he knew she would be there. "Once or twice. I can't really recall." On that note he closed his eyes and lay back on the lounge chair.

"You're a lousy liar, Matthew Relic," Corinne informed him with a smile in her heart. Then she remembered her mother's strategy lessons and lay down beside him, her hand ever so softly brushing against his.

Matthew felt the brush of her hand and couldn't resist. He opened his palm and captured her fingers in between his, then closed his hand around hers in case she thought of escaping.

Corinne considered this development. This wasn't exactly how it was supposed to work. Her mother said casual touches to distract him and keep him waiting for the next brush or touch. If he was holding her hand the whole time, how could he be thinking of the next touch when the first touch never ended? But she supposed it did feel good to lie there next to him, connected. So she decided it was all right for now.

They slept together that way. Arm-to-arm. Hand-in-hand. Fingers entwined. A soft breeze wafted over their bodies and the sound of the ocean lulled them into unconsciousness. People milled about; children could be heard laughing and frolicking in the water.

And the hot sun continued to hang high above their heads.

7

"Ow," Matthew groaned as he tried to move his legs. The skin covering his shins felt tight and hot almost as if he'd been...burned!

Matthew sat up immediately and gauged the position of the sun. It was well past noon. Closer to maybe three or four judging by the sun's slow descent. Which meant that he and Rinny had been exposed to its powerful rays since late morning.

Matthew could see his thighs and shins below his bathing trunks. He did a cooked lobster justice. Inspecting his arms, he found them in a similar state. When he tried to bend his elbow, he feared the skin might actually rip like cheap paper.

"Rinny," he said trying to wake her.

He didn't dare touch her. The one piece and the sarong had saved her most of her body. But her arms and the bottom of her legs were as red as his. If she wanted to, she could probably fry an egg on her bare thigh. Somehow Matthew doubted that she would want to.

Luckily for her, the impossibly large hat she wore covered most of her face and shoulders. But the wind must have pushed back the left brim a bit, exposing a patch of her cheek that he could see was a vibrant shade of scarlet.

The other side of her hat, though, had, he noted thankfully, shaded his face as well. He lifted his hand to his right cheek and winced. At least it had protected half of his face. He could only imagine what he looked like. Images of the comic strip figure Two-Face floated through his mind. Well, look at the bright side, he thought, no pun intended, at least he and Rinny would be a matched set.

"Rinny, wake up. Come on, Rinny. We've got to get out of the sun."

Corinne stirred. She'd been having such a delightful dream. Matthew was kissing her neck and trailing his hand down her throat and over her breast and the fluttery feeling in her stomach was turning into something more urgent. "Matthew," she breathed.

Then, as if she'd heard the sound of her own voice, heard the huskiness and the plea, she sat up abruptly. She'd been dreaming about the wrong man. Maybe Matthew was the man she was prepared to trust with her body, but she couldn't forget who had already claimed her heart.

It was... His name was... Oh, my goodness! She forgot his name. It was right there. Right on the tip of her tongue, something with a B....

Brendan. Phew, she sighed in relief.

She wasn't fickle. She wouldn't be fickle. She'd said she loved Brendan. She'd told him and the world as much. Corinne was going to stick by that declaration come hell or high water. Or Matthew.

"Rinny, we've got to get out of the sun. We're both burned to a crisp."

It wasn't until he said those words that Corinne felt a distinct stinging all over her lower body. Looking down at herself she could see the patterns of red along her skin. Her sarong covered one hip and thigh, but the material separated partly over her left thigh and leg, leaving it exposed.

And this particular sarong had tassels on the bottom. When she lifted the skirt, she could see where the sun had burned the pattern of the tassels into her skin.

"Ahh!" she shouted. But in doing so, she found the patch of burned skin on her left cheek and raised her hand to it.

"Are you in that much pain?" Matthew asked, his voice laced with concern for her pain.

"It's not the pain, it's the pattern," she cried. Red and white lines crisscrossed her skin, making it appear that she had some freakish tattoo emblazoned on her leg.

Gingerly, Matthew stood. He offered a hand to Corinne and lifted her out of the lounge chair slowly. Together they hobbled their way up the beach, to a chorus of oohs, aahhs, ows and hisses as their limbs protested any movement that required their skin to stretch.

When they reached the lobby of the hotel, Corinne could feel the eyes of the other tourists and locals upon her. There was sympathy, but there was also the silent question of how they had let such a thing happen. Everyone knew about sunblock these days.

Never one to shy away from the public eye, she explained to the onlookers, "We fell asleep."

Waves of pity emanated about them. Because everyone knew, everyone except them, of course, that they were not in for a very pleasant evening. They took the elevator up to Corinne's room. Once inside the room Matthew headed straight for the bathroom. The bathtub was a step-in tub and large enough to fit the both of them. He turned on the water and checked to see that the temperature was only moderately cool, just enough to take the sting out of their burns.

"Follow me," he called out to her.

Corinne stood in the bathroom door and watched as the tub filled up with water. She stood back while Matthew, still in his bathing suit and T-shirt, stepped into the tub, sighing as the cool water washed over his overheated skin.

"This feels much better. Come on," he encouraged.

For a moment she hesitated as she contemplated the knot of the sarong at her hip.

"Rinny, I saw everything there was to see last night. The food poisoning didn't affect my memory at all," Matthew explained logically.

Point taken. She dropped the sarong and followed him into the tub. "Oooh, oooh," she moaned as the water practically turned to steam when it hit her limbs. Taking a seat on the ledge next to Matthew she submerged herself to her shoulders in the water.

Once comfortable, she turned to check on Matthew. He looked like a clown in half makeup. One side of his face was neon-red while the other was flesh-white. The laughter began to bubble inside her and once it started to spill out, she couldn't stop it.

Only she had to because the left side of her face hurt too much to continue laughing.

"You're all heart," he said sarcastically, but it was impossible to be really angry at her mirth. After all, he'd caught a glimpse of himself in the mirror. "We don't seem to be having a great deal of luck."

That was the understatement of the millennium. But it did sober her up. "Maybe this," she returned, waving her hand between the two of them, "wasn't meant to be."

"No," Matthew stated insistently. "I refuse to believe

that. A few minor setbacks, that's all. Have no fear, Rinny. I'll take your revirginity yet!"

The seriousness of his tone sent her into another round of giggles. "Oh, Matthew," she breathed through her hysteria, "we make quite a team." She reached out to touch his arm, but quickly backed off when she heard him hiss.

So much for step two in her mother's lesson of man seduction. Casual touching didn't do much good when you sent the person you were touching into a chorus of hisses.

"Here," she began, "why don't you take off this shirt. It's brushing against your arms and irritating the burn." So saying, Rinny moved closer to him and gently reached under the water to pull his shirt off.

Matthew tried to raise his arms over his head while she pulled the material over his body but was only able to get them halfway there. It was close enough, apparently, because Rinny was able to negotiate the wet cotton over his back and head. He heard a thump as it hit the bathroom floor.

Then he heard her gasp.

Damn, he'd forgotten about the stupid scar. She wasn't supposed to see it until she was so aroused that she wouldn't be able to see anything through the desire clouding her eyes. No chance of that happening now.

Matthew watched her as she stared at his chest. The scar cut across his pec in the vicinity of his heart. A vicious mark, it was raised and puckered, but smooth to the touch. His chest hair had just started growing back and would no doubt eventually cover the thing, but for now it was exposed to anyone looking. And Rinny was looking.

Matthew started to move. His intent was to leave the

tub and snatch up his shirt, but Rinny moved off her seat to kneel in front of him. She stopped him dead in his tracks by closing her palm over his chest.

"Does it hurt?"

"No," he uttered past the lump that had formed in his throat.

Carefully, she trailed her fingertip around the edge of the puckered skin. It ran vertically over his chest then curved at the bottom. The bullet hadn't left this mark. This was the mark of the surgeon's knife that had cut Matthew open to extract the metal lodged so dangerously close to his heart. So close.

"What if I lost you?" she asked of no one in particular. The pain of what might have been was suddenly too much to bear.

"You didn't." Matthew reached for the hand that covered his heart and pulled it to his lips. Reverently, he kissed the tips of the fingers that had traced his scar, grateful for the pleasure they gave in a place that had suffered so much pain.

"Why didn't you want me to see the scar?" Corinne wondered, as Matthew finished giving thanks to her hand and laid it on his unburned cheek.

"It's ugly," he explained simply.

"Ugly!" she shouted, suddenly enraged. "Do you think I care? Do you think I'm so shallow that I would be repulsed by a scar? Do you think appearances are all that is important to me?"

Corinne pulled her hand from his cheek, but Matthew caught it with his own. "No," he answered. "No, I don't think you're shallow. And no, I don't think appearances are important to you. Ironic don't you think, since you seem to be under the impression that they are important to all the people around you. Do you deny it?"

She opened her mouth to say something, then closed it. "No. But it's different for me."

"Why?"

"Because I'm a Weatherby. People expect me to be glamorous like my mother. Beautiful like my sister. You can't understand what a disappointment I was to them when I turned out to be..." Corinne was at a loss for words.

But Matthew wasn't. "What? Beautiful, smart, funny, bright, independent. I can imagine their shock and dismay."

She smiled, but with no humor. "I wasn't an actress."

"You could have been if you wanted to be," he argued. "You're talented. You just chose to use that talent in other ways. And your gift with numbers is not something you should take lightly. Hell, if it weren't for that gift, your family would probably be in financial ruin by now. I know all about the work you do for them. Are they aware of how grateful they should be to you?"

It was a stirring speech. Corinne couldn't help but marvel at his vehemence. Matthew was bound and determined to defend her to...herself. It was the sweetest thing anyone had ever done for her. For a moment she tried to picture Brendan standing with her in a tub of cold water while they soaked away their burns. She tried to imagine what he would say when she confessed her family's disappointment with her.

Probably something along the lines of that she should have gone into films because she could really have cleaned up on her name alone. He'd suggested as much in the past.

A tight fist formed around her heart. For the first time Corinne began to realize how those words had hurt her. Worse, she was beginning to wonder why she would have handed over her heart to a man who treated it so cruelly and caused her pain more often than not.

But she had handed it over. It was gone now, and she couldn't take it back. Not unless she wanted to start herself on a pattern of meaningless love affairs that seemed to run in her family as much as dramatics did.

No. She refused to walk down that path. There was only going to be one love. One lover. Well, two counting Matthew. Because there *was* going to be Matthew.

And Danny, and that dork from college, and Carlos...but they didn't count.

Corinne slid up against him. The water lapped against their heated skin. Again, she closed her palm over his wounded heart. "I'm glad you finally trusted me enough to let me see it."

He wanted to refute her statement that letting her see his wound had anything to do with trust, but it would have been a lie. The scar, to him, was proof of a lot of things. His stupidity. His vulnerability. Maybe his courage. But in a contest, courage lost to stupidity. It wasn't something he wanted everyone to see. But he was glad that Rinny had.

Lowering his face he touched her lips with his. Again. And again. Then again. He pulled her up against his body, wanting the total contact of her against him as he'd never wanted anything before. But he couldn't prevent the hiss that escaped his lips when her legs brushed against his own.

"Oh," she returned, feeling the same sting herself.

Matthew adjusted his position so that their legs were separated by at least an inch and fought the pain in his arms as he tried to hold her, because the pleasure was too compelling. Her mouth was hot and wet. Her taste was ripe and fresh like a fruit, although unlike any fruit he'd ever eaten. She was a drug that he wanted to become addicted to for the rest of his life.

He lifted his head and aimed for the curve of her neck, his hand cupping her cheek to hold her still.

"Ow," she cried out and gripped his forearms, which in turn made him wince.

"Let's try this again," he murmured against her throat, careful to keep his hands at a safe distance. He dropped his mouth to the soft white mound that peaked over her bathing-suit top, his tongue running along the edge. Then he fell to his knees and let the water rise up to his chest. He reached for her thighs, intending to pull her down to join him and heard her screech.

Resigned, he sighed.

Corinne patted his head. "I'm sorry. It's okay. Keep going." It had felt really good right up to the point where he had touched her burned skin.

It wasn't okay. Matthew stood in the water and took a step back; his hands held up in front of him to prevent them from touching any more of her damaged skin. After a few calming breaths, he spoke. "This isn't going to work."

"It's okay," she protested. "It's really not that bad."

Painfully, Matthew smiled. "I don't want it to be 'not bad.' I want it to be wonderful. Let's get out of the tub. I'll order us up some room service and some body lotion. I'm sure the concierge will have just the thing to take the sting out. Tomorrow we will be right as rain."

"Tomorrow," she agreed longingly.

"Tomorrow," he said finally.

SITTING ON THE BED, Corinne in a loose-fitting robe and Matthew wrapped in a towel, they devoured the pizza that room service had delivered and that was hotter than they were and drank a few bottles of beer between them to numb the pain.

"Tell me," Corinne chuckled as she squeezed out another dollop of soothing lotion onto her palm.

Matthew was stretched out on the bed, his back against the headboard, as he followed the path Corinne's slathered hands took. Slowly, she lowered her hands to his leg and began to rub the lotion in carefully and thoroughly, leaving no part of his burnt leg untouched.

So thoroughly that he forgot the question she had asked him.

"Come on," she prompted. "You know you can't lie. You have painted me, haven't you?"

"All right," he confessed, then purred when her cream-covered hands reached his upper thigh.

Sensing she wasn't going to get a coherent answer if she continued toward her current destination, Corinne pulled her hands away just before she attempted to snake her fingers under the terry-cloth towel. Technically, the higher up she went the less burned he was. Still, it was a heady thought to know that she could drive this man to sexual distraction. That he wanted her was beyond doubt and she hadn't even gotten to her mother's lesson number five!

She applied another blob of cream to her palms and started again with his other leg.

With Rinny once again in ankle territory, Matthew was able to think. "I just don't think you'll like it. It's sort of abstract."

"Abstract?"

"That's what all of us artists say who have no real talent and can't replicate what we see in life," Matthew told her. "But it's you. You were in my thoughts when I did it."

"When did you do it?" she wondered.

"A few years ago. Why?"

Years. That was long before the shooting. Long before she assumed his crush for her had begun. Had he been thinking of her that long? And if he had, could it really be termed a crush? Something that lasted years was usually called...love.

Did Matthew love her? Is that why he had followed her to this island? The power of that conclusion punched her in the chest and made it difficult to breathe. It was one thing to have an affair with a man who had a crush on her. But it was a very different thing to have an affair with a man who loved her. Love wasn't something that should be treated casually. It needed to be revered, treasured. Above all, respected.

Soberly, she pulled her hands away from his leg.

"Done?" he inquired, a note of disappointment in his voice.

Corinne heard the disappointment. "I think I got everywhere," she told him, distracted now by thoughts of love.

Matthew sensed her distance and wondered about it. Two minutes ago they'd been giddy as children, but now Corinne looked as if she were puzzling the mysteries of life. "Rinny?"

"Hmm?"

He wanted to ask what was wrong, but decided not to push. Things had been going so well for them, except, of course, for her hangover, his food poisoning and their sunburns. But other than that he was having the time of his life. If Rinny needed a little time to think, then that was the least he could do for her. "Well, I'd better be going," he announced.

"Going?" she asked, suddenly snapped out of her musings. "But last night you stayed over." It was one of things she was most looking forward to this night. Mind-blowing exhilarating passion was the first thing, naturally, but a close second to that was being held in a pair of large arms just as she'd been held the night before.

"Last night we weren't both suffering from near-second-degree burns. Trust me, you don't want me anywhere near you tonight," he said as he gingerly threw his legs off the bed and stood. He made his way to the bathroom where his clothes were drying and returned a second later in his suit and T-shirt.

His point was debatable, but she supposed the time to herself might be good for her. She needed to think through this idea that Matthew might actually be in love with her, and what that meant for them and their affair. "Okay. I guess I'll see you tomorrow then?"

"Sure. No beach for us though. Maybe we should hit the casinos."

Gambling, she mused. She might as well. After all, she had agreed to take the biggest risk of her life since she'd arrived on this island. A little more risk wouldn't make much of a difference. "I'll be there."

Leaning over, Matthew pecked her lips lightly. Anything else and they would end up back where they had been in the tub, hissing and wincing at each other.

Funny, Corinne thought, but the simple peck on her lips seemed more proprietary than any deep kiss Brendan had ever given her. When Matthew reluctantly pulled away and left the room, she ran her tongue over her lips to see if she could taste what she suspected was already there.

Yep. It tasted a lot like love.

LATE THE NEXT AFTERNOON, after a morning spent in the hair salon in an attempt to detract from the red blotch on her cheek with perfectly fabulous hair, Corinne made her way down to the casino. The burn had settled down to a minor annoyance, but in deference to her tender skin, and in consideration of the still-ridiculous tan lines she now sported, she wore a flowing white skirt that brushed against her ankles as she moved, and a matching poet's blouse that billowed with each step. The affect was supposed to be angelic.

Virginal. It was the first thought that came to his mind. Matthew was seated at a table filled with other men, staring at cards that he was pretty sure would ensure him the pot of money in the center of the table, when he spotted a flowing white goddess gliding across the room.

Not for long, he decided. Tonight was definitely the night. Rinny's revirginity was history. He was taking no chances. No drinks for either of them. No sun. No suspicious-looking food. No sharp instruments. No to anything that might in some way interfere with what he knew was going to be the greatest night of passion he'd ever known.

Part of him wanted to leave the poker table, swing her up into his arms, and march them both to bed before anything else could happen. But they had come too far and he had waited too long to act impulsively now. They both deserved a romantic evening with all the trappings. That meant candlelight, soft music, dancing and finally, soft wet kisses that would strip away any reservations that still lingered.

As if she could hone in on his lustful thoughts, Matthew watched as Corinne scanned the crowd searching for him. He lifted a hand to help her out and watched as her curious expression turned into something more like annoyance.

Hands planted firmly on her hips she made her way through the crowd to his table. "Matthew, what are you doing?"

"Waiting for a lucky kiss from my girl."

The four other men at his table, two on their ten-year-anniversary trip, the other two on their twenty-fifth-year-anniversary trip, groaned in unison.

"Hey, we said no honeymooners at this table," Bud, the statesman of the group, objected.

"What's wrong with honeymooners?" Corinne asked, slightly offended although she couldn't imagine why.

Bud snorted and closed his five cards into one. "Because honeymooners talk that love crap all day. It gets in the way of us men trying to play a decent hand of cards."

Appropriately, Corinne gasped at the use of the word *love* and *crap* in the same sentence. "I will have you know that love is the most beautiful, most special thing in this world. All of you only wish your wives were around to give you good-luck kisses."

The group mumbled their assent.

Then Bud asked of Matthew, "Are you going to bid or not?"

"Yes."

"No," Corinne countered.

"But..." Matthew began.

Resolutely, she shook her head. "Matthew, you know

you can't play poker. You have no capacity for lying. I'm sure these men are only using you as a duck."

"Duck?"

"Swan?" she tried again. When that didn't sound right, she amended with, "Parakeet?"

"Pigeon!" Bud interjected. "The word is *pigeon*."

"I thought pigeons were snitchers," Matthew added.

"Regardless," Corinne stated, "it's time we were going. Before you lose any more money."

"But I was winning," Matthew protested.

Under her breath, which was ridiculous because the table was small enough for the other men to hear everything she said anyway, Corinne whispered, "That's what they do. They let you win a few hands before they take you for the big bucks. It's called sprinkling."

"Seeding!" Bud shouted. "It's called seeding."

Corinne shot him a nasty look and left it at that.

"Just let me play out this hand, sweetheart."

She sighed and glanced over his shoulder. "But, Matthew honey, with all of those aces you're never going to get close to twenty-one."

"Fold."

"Fold."

"I fold."

"I'm out."

Closing his eyes, Matthew took a moment to remind himself that he was in love with the woman who had no doubt cost him a few hundred dollars. "We weren't playing twenty-one," he uttered between clenched teeth.

Innocently, she raised her brow. "You weren't?"

Matthew wasn't buying it for a moment. "Okay, you win." He gathered up the meager pot and dropped his cards on the table. "Thanks for the game, guys."

As they walked away from the table, Matthew was sure he heard Bud curse all honeymooners.

"You didn't really want to keep playing, did you?" Corinne asked in a tone that suggested the only answer she wanted was one that affirmed her previous opinion.

It was a battle he wasn't going to win. Besides, she did call him honey. For a consolation prize it wasn't bad. "No. I wanted to be with you."

Said so honestly, with no hint of sarcasm or insincerity, his words pierced her heart. That he loved her was so clear. So obvious. She'd been a fool to have missed it all these months. All these years! But now that the cat was out of the bag she wasn't sure how to proceed. Part of her knew the only fair thing to do would be to confront his feelings head-on and warn him that his love could never be reciprocated.

But only part. The other part of her wanted to be with him, too. What did that mean?

Conflict. It was the cornerstone of every tragedy. Fortunately, Corinne excelled at tragedies.

"So what do you want to do next?" Matthew queried.

"It's getting late. How about a cocktail and some dinner?"

Matthew took a quick glance at his apparel. Khakis and a green polo. It wasn't necessarily dinner attire. He patted his pocket. No tissues either.

"Come on," Corinne encouraged. "You look fine. We'll eat at the outside restaurant again. Safe food and casual attire."

Since he didn't want to take the time to change, he agreed. And besides, he was beginning to like life without a tie strapped around his neck. Corinne was making a world of changes in his normally staid life. He could feel himself becoming a little wilder, a little more reckless. Next thing he knew he'd be packing turkey for lunch instead of bologna.

Dinner turned out to be snacks instead of real food. Corinne didn't want a heavy meal weighing her down this night, but she didn't want her stomach to be growling either so she ate a third nacho.

"You promise me you're not mad about this afternoon? I suppose you have a right to be. I did come off pretty high-handed. Which is strange because that's really not me at all."

Matthew had to work to smother a chortle.

He didn't succeed. "I'm not *that* bad!" Corinne protested. "However, I recognize that I did sort of sound like your wife."

A fact that didn't bother Matthew at all. "What's a few hundred dollars? Actually it was probably closer to three hundred dollars. Then if you take into account my other winnings, I would have been up almost four hundred, fifty-six dollars and ninety-two cents. Plus there was the slot machine I played and..."

"Matthew!" Corinne interrupted.

"Off script again?"

"You're supposed to agree that I'm not that bad."

"Oh, yes, I mean no. I mean I'm not mad and you're not bad. I was just counting."

"I see."

"No more, I promise. It's the accountant in me. When the numbers enter my head sometimes I have to count them before they leave. But enough about boring numbers."

"I don't think numbers are boring," Corinne corrected him.

That's right. She was a numbers lady. For the first time Matthew didn't have to apologize for who he was. It was liberating. And it was just one more reason why he loved her. He imagined them having a long life of loving and counting. It was going to be great.

"Let's dance," he announced.

"Matthew..."

"Wait!" He held his hand up to prevent interruption. "For the last few nights you've tried to convince me that I don't know how to dance. But I know something you don't know."

He didn't immediately tell her what that was and the suspense was so unlike him, it made her smile. She was rubbing off on him more and more each day. "Well?" she encouraged.

"I know how to dance."

"You do?" she asked skeptically.

Slightly affronted at the skepticism he heard, Matthew repeated, "I do. My mother was a dancing instructor. Granted, I didn't spend a lot of time in her studio, but I was able to dance the basic steps before I could walk. Satisfied?"

Rather than answer, she stood and offered her hand to him. He grasped it and tucked it under his elbow. "We're off."

The dance floor was crowded with couples swaying to the calypso beat. The tempo was slow, but not slow enough for Matthew to pull Rinny against him until she melted into his body the way he wanted to. Nor was it fast enough to spin her about and start her blood pumping in an excited frenzy.

Either situation would be ideal for the remainder of the night's activities.

"Wait here," he told her and went in search of the bandleader. The man on stage leading the small band sported dreadlocks, a floral-print shirt and an easy island manner. When Matthew approached, he leaned over to take his request. After a nod, Matthew was satisfied he would have his wish.

As he began to make his way back to where he'd left Rinny, Matthew heard the beat starting to pick up.

Reaching Rinny, he wrapped a strong arm about her waist and caught her other hand in his. "Ready?"

The twinkle in his eyes was infectious, and it made her heart pound before they even took the first step. He waited for the beat and then he moved her. It wasn't quite dancing. Corinne would have had to be participating in order for it to be dancing. Instead she just followed while Matthew led her about the floor in tight controlled moves that made her cheeks flush and her heart race.

She couldn't believe it. He was a master on the floor, shifting slightly to guide her, controlling her movements without bullying her. It was all she could do to keep up, and she had had her share of dance lessons as well. For a brief moment, Corinne felt caught in the middle of a Fred Astaire movie. Only, Ginger she was not!

But it didn't matter. After a few spins, dips, twists and turns, Corinne knew she could trust Matthew entirely to lead the way. All she had to do was hang on and not trip. It was exhilarating to be so free. To feel him release her into a spin and know that when she came out of it, he would be right there to catch her. To feel him dip her so close to the floor, but be assured that he would never let her drop.

It was one of those moments of pure joy and happiness that a person very rarely recognized until it was over. Corinne was determined not to make that mistake. She was going to seize the moment. Let it burn in her brain so that she would never forget this moment, this night, this man.

She took in the plentiful stars above, the sound of the rhythmic music pounding in time, it seemed, with her heart, the heat emanating from the crowd that surrounded them, and Matthew. It was all too good to be true.

Suddenly the music ended. Corinne found herself caught up against his body. Her face inches from his, puffs of breaths that she couldn't seem to control hitting his lips. Vaguely, she heard applause, and out of her peripheral vision she could see that the crowd had formed an open circle around them.

What a show they had been, she thought, followed by the realization that for the first time she had been the center of attention, a position she typically craved, and she hadn't even been aware of it. She hadn't been aware of anything except Matthew. His arms, his strength and all the trust she afforded him.

Oblivious to the crowd and tempted beyond any control, Corinne swayed forward and closed the remaining distance between them. His lips were warm and soft, but she felt them go firm as his mouth closed over hers. His tongue pushed its way inside her mouth and she felt the intensity of his need.

It was like no other kiss before, and she couldn't imagine that anything similar could ever happen after. It wasn't just the kiss. It was the moment. It was the span of time when they stood suspended on the dance floor, invisible, or so they thought, to the world around them, while they merged together. They breathed the same air. Shared the same space. Communicated with lips and tongues while their souls did all the talking.

Finally, Matthew regained his senses and pushed

himself away from her before he took her on the floor in front of anyone who wanted to watch. The applause had grown louder and he didn't think it had anything to do with their fine dancing performance.

"Rinny."

Dazed, her head bobbed about on her shoulders. When she finally stopped spinning and was able to open her eyes all she saw was him. Not surprising, considering he had her tiny body hauled up against his massive frame.

But seeing wasn't about sight all the time. Corinne wasn't just looking at Matthew. She was peering deep inside him all the way to his toes, and the truth was, it was shaking the foundation that she had stood on for so many months with Brendan.

This man loved her, at least that was what his kiss told her, and she felt so strongly for him that she was having a hard time deciphering where friendship ended and love began.

But Matthew gave her no more time to think about it. Instead he leaned down and swept her off her feet to another round of applause from the crowd.

"Oh my," she whispered against his lips. "I think I might faint."

"Oh, no you don't," he insisted. "Not this time. We need to get to your room. Quick!"

He carried her through the crowd with everyone shouting their approval—not to mention a few suggestions—along the way.

As Matthew reached the end of the dance floor with his prize still in his arms, he heard the woman next to him exclaim, "How romantic!"

The man standing next to her, whom Matthew recognized as Bud from the poker game earlier, replied, "Just don't expect that kind of stuff from me. I've got a sensitive hernia. Damn honeymooners...they give all of us regular guys a bad name."

8

MATTHEW CARRIED Rinny from the dance floor, all the way back to the hotel, through the lobby and even while they rode the elevator up to Corinne's floor. It was very reminiscent of their first night together, only this time she was sober and not sneezing.

This helped to enhance the mood.

The doors slid open and Matthew made his way to her door. "The key?" he asked.

Corinne, who had been in a minor stupor since having her soul sucked out of her by his kiss, repeated dully, "The key?"

"The key," Matthew said. "It opens the door."

"The door to my heart is already open." She sighed dramatically.

That was pleasant to hear, but it did little to help him open the door. "Let's try another approach. We'll go to my room."

If his arms were beginning to ache at all he didn't think about it. There was no way he was putting Corinne down. No doubt she would fall and sprain her ankle or twist her wrist on impact or something else that would prevent this night from happening.

And it was going to happen. Even if it killed him.

Matthew marched back down the hall and stood at the elevator. "Hit the button," he told Corinne, whose hands were more accessible.

"Yes," she whispered into his ear, her head resting against his shoulder. "You hit the magical button inside my soul."

Okay. That was definitely a plus, but it wasn't going to open the elevator doors.

Matthew twisted his body and shifted her weight a bit so he could jab at the button. Only the light didn't go on. He hit it again, harder this time. Still no light. He looked up at the illuminated numbers above the door and saw that the numbers two and three were both lit but they weren't moving.

"Elevator's stuck," he said to no one in particular since Corinne still looked to be enmeshed in some sort of love spell. Since it was his kiss that had put her there, he couldn't fault her for it. "Plan B. The stairs."

The door to the stairs was just around the corner. Again, Matthew found it necessary to shift Rinny higher up into his arms so he could turn the knob. Once it was opened he looked at the steep steps leading up before him. Five floors worth if he was doing the math right.

"Here, let's try this," he said, moving Rinny about in his arms, and shifting her so that by the time they were done she was sprawled on his back, her legs were around his waist, and she was riding him piggy-back fashion.

Waking from her temporary daze, Corinne took note of their situation. It was sort of kinky, she concluded, but not very romantic. Fortunately for them, she had regained enough of her senses to suggest the obvious. "Matthew, put me down. I can walk."

"No!" he barked. "You're not walking. I'm not taking any chances."

Not wanting to put up a fight, and not wanting to lose

contact with Matthew, she shrugged and locked her legs more securely about his waist.

He groaned and it echoed off the walls of the stairwell.

"Too tight?" she wondered.

"No," he muttered. Not tight enough.

The feel of her legs wrapped around him made him think of other positions they might be in where her legs would be tightly wrapped around him. Lustful positions. Matthew groaned again, but this time silently because the echo in the stairwell was really loud and he didn't want to let on to Corinne, or anyone else who might be listening, that he was on the verge of ravishing her.

Two flights, an aching back and straining lungs later, Matthew headed for the exit and emerged from the stairwell. "Maybe the elevator is working by now," he suggested, his breath backing up on him.

He made his way through the hall over to the elevator doors and hit the button, much easier this time with Rinny on his back, rather than in his arms. This time the light lit up and he could watch the floors blink to life as the elevator lifted itself to them. The bell sounded and the doors opened.

Matthew stepped inside and the doors closed behind him. He turned and hit the appropriate button on the panel. There was a momentary grinding noise, but eventually the elevator started to move upwards. He might have been worried about such a noise had it not been for the quick kisses Rinny was placing on various spots on his neck. She would swoop down from behind him and her lips would make contact with his skin. Just those tiny little touches were enough to start his heart beating more rapidly.

"Rinny, if you don't stop, I'm going to lose control."

Matthew out of control. Now that was an interesting proposition. Wondering exactly how much it would take, Corinne dove down for another attack. This time she fastened her teeth around his earlobe and bit down. Hard enough to get his attention.

A manly moan filled the elevator. "I warned you."

In a smooth series of coordinated moves, that very much resembled the dance he had performed earlier that evening, Matthew dropped her legs and let them slide down his body. Instantly, he twisted in the arms that were still wrapped around his neck and captured Rinny's lips in a heated kiss.

Corinne could only marvel at the power of the man in her arms. There was such passion behind his sober expressions. Underneath his tissue-filled breast pocket lurked the heart of Don Juan, Romeo and Casanova all rolled into one. She could only hang on while he ravished her mouth. His tongue penetrated her lips and teeth and sought hers in another kind of dance. A move he performed just as skillfully as the steps he'd taught her earlier.

"We have to stop," she gasped as she tried to gain control of her heart and body. She feared both were already long gone at the mercy of Matthew's stunning virility, but she still had a semblance of sense. "What if the doors open?"

As if on cue, a loud grinding noise filled the tight box. Clunk. Clunk. Clunk. Cluunnnnk! Silence.

"I don't think we have to worry about the doors opening anytime soon." Lasciviously, Matthew wiggled his brows.

Then the time for play was over as he hauled Rinny back up against his body. Her small curves molded to the hard planes of his chest and thighs. She seemed to melt into him. Simultaneously, he kissed a path around her neck while with his hands he kneaded her plump buttocks beneath her flowing skirt.

Desperate for complete contact, he pulled her hips tighter against his so she would know how much he wanted her, understand how long he had waited and guess that he couldn't wait much longer.

"Matthew," she breathed as the air rushed out of her lungs at the feel of his hardness against her belly and the touch of his tongue at the base of her throat. The contrast of soft and hard sent thrills up her spine and turned the once tickly feelings in her stomach to all-out urges.

Those urges were telling her more. More kisses, more contact, more Matthew. It had been a long time since she'd been with a man, but she recognized the need to have Matthew fill her deep inside almost immediately. That desire was more than irresistible.

It was almost frightening. She didn't think she could wait any longer. "Please, Matthew. Now!"

His sentiments exactly. The last place he wanted to take Rinny for the first time was in a public elevator. But when she stepped back from him and began unbuttoning the buttons on her poet's blouse, revealing beneath it a transparent bra that did more to showcase her breasts than to cover them, he figured...what the hell!

With no padding this time, the small round curves of her breasts fitted perfectly into his palms. Matthew brushed each nipple with his index finger, turning the already hardened peaks solid.

"I need to kiss them," he said to no one in particular.

Reaching into the open material of her blouse, he unfastened her bra so that it hung loosely off her shoulders. His hands tested the soft flesh of her back and circled her body until her bare breasts were nestled into his palms once more, this time with no barrier between his hands and her skin. No longer able to withstand the temptation he lowered his head and replaced his hands with his mouth.

Her first thought was that he was going to try and swallow her whole. Which would have been fine with her because she had come to the irrational conclusion that she could live quite happily inside Matthew's hot wet mouth for the rest of her days. Instead, he closed his teeth over the peak of her breast, which sent a direct shock to the center of her belly...and lower.

She did the only sane thing any rational woman could do. She grabbed onto his head to hold him in place so that she would never lose this delicious sensation, dropped her head back on her shoulders, and screamed.

Quickly, Matthew raised his head to cover her mouth with his own and swallow her screams before she notified the whole building of their activities inside the stalled elevator. Only, once he had her mouth under his, he remembered what a thrill it was to plunge inside her heat again and again with his tongue. In turn, that reminded him that there was somewhere else he wanted to be plunging inside. Again and again.

Lifting her in his arms he lowered them both to the floor of the elevator, careful to keep her on top of him.

When she realized she was straddled over his lap, she smiled wickedly. "Don't you like to be on top?"

"Sometimes," he panted. "But this is our first time, and I don't want to take you on the floor of the elevator. Seems a little crass. However, I don't see a problem as long as you're not touching the floor. Agreed?"

"Agreed," she concurred lustfully.

She shucked off her blouse and let the bra fall from her arms. Then she pulled the skirt over her head as the elastic waist stretched to accommodate her body. When it was gone, all that separated them were the briefest pair of panties Matthew had ever had the good fortune to see. That and his khakis and polo shirt.

Corinne went for the shirt first. She pulled it out of the waist of his pants and pushed it high over his chest, revealing a thick mat of hair and muscle as well as his scar.

While Matthew helped her to remove the shirt completely she lowered herself over him and touched her lips ever so gently to the puckered skin.

"What are you doing?" he whispered as he watched the erotic scene unfold before his eyes.

"I'm kissing it and making it all better," she returned. Then she carefully applied her lips to every inch of the jagged mark, kissing him softly so that he would feel how much she cared for him. That task complete, she moved on to his nipples, which were also puckered, but for a very different reason.

"You already made me better," he told her sincerely, although he doubted she would hear him, as engrossed in her task as she was.

But Corinne did hear him. And the nibbling fear that maybe his love for her was nothing more than an extension of gratitude returned. Something inside her heart was shifting. Maybe it had started to happen when she had looked up and seen his face above hers that first day on the beach. Maybe it had happened when he had held her head as she puked up her guts. Maybe it had happened when they had danced, so smoothly, so elegantly together. Or maybe it was his kiss.

Corinne couldn't say for sure, but she knew that she wanted him to love her. Needed it, in fact. And it had to be real love. Not born out of something so pathetic as gratitude.

She lifted herself on his lap and met his eyes. Blue eyes stared back at her so intently, she might have guessed he was gazing straight through her. Corinne reached for the snap of his pants, and, as gently as she could, she lowered the zipper. Resting her weight on her knees on either side of his hips, she pushed the pants and his boxers off his hips and down his thighs. He helped her by kicking the material away.

Naked, he was a god. Which was slightly intimidating considering she was just…a woman. Hesitantly, she touched his thick erection and started when it seemed to jump in her hand. Poor Matthew had his eyes closed in what she feared might be agony, but based on the sounds he was making Corinne had to conclude it was pleasure. Deep pleasure that rocked him to the very soles of his feet if his muttered words were to be believed.

She shucked her own panties and moved back over him so that sex touched sex.

"Matthew," she whispered.

In an instant he raised himself so they were chest to chest. He skimmed her cheek with his hand and touched her lips with his fingers. "Ready?"

"Yes," she choked out.

"We'll take it slow."

He lowered his hands to her hips and lifted her onto his sex. He pushed gently but insistently inside her, waiting as her body gradually opened itself to his penetration. Her slick sheath eased his way along. Then after a moment, their eyes joined, Matthew finished the connection by joining their bodies completely in one deep thrust.

The sensation was like nothing she had ever felt before. She was right, she thought dimly, none of those other lovers counted. Only Matthew. Only now.

He filled her near to bursting. So much so, it might have been painful if Matthew hadn't been kissing her cheek, brushing his tongue against her earlobe, whispering words of encouragement to her as he moved deep inside her. Instead it was a glorious experience. So pure, so raw, that there was really only one thing for her to do. For the second time, she let her head fall back and her throat arch and screamed in delightful abandon.

This time Matthew let her scream. If she was feeling a tenth of what he was, then he couldn't blame her. And if he hadn't been concentrating so hard on breathing, he might have joined her. Instead he sucked in air to keep his heart pumping, and with his hands at her hips lifted Corinne ever so slightly on his shaft so he could lower her and once again sink deep inside her warmth.

Home. It wasn't the sexiest thought a man in his position could have, but it was a true one. Inside her, with her arms wrapped around his neck and her voice scratchy from shouting with pleasure, Matthew knew a contentedness he'd never known before. This woman was made for him and because they fit so well together he knew the same was true for her.

The question was, after the passion faded, would she recognize that truth?

The easy solution was never to let the passion fade. But as her movements above him became more frantic, he sensed she was nearing a conclusion. One that he was anxious to join her in. He felt her muscles tighten deliciously around his shaft and it pushed him over the edge. He thrust deep and let himself go in a way he had never dreamed he could.

"Matthew!" she screamed again, as colorful lights

burst behind her eyes. It was the strangest experience. It was as if for the first time she truly felt all of her body. Inside and out.

A shame, she decided, that she should feel it at the end like this because she was certain she was dying. Her body was exploding and imploding. Her muscles were contracting and expanding. Soon she would collapse entirely and that would be the end of her.

But it was okay. She would die with Matthew on her mind and in her heart and in her body. Corinne dropped her head against Matthew's chest. The heart that had cheated death, pounded heavily against her cheek. It was a glorious way to die.

"Hold tight, ma'am! We're going to get you out!"

Funny, Corinne thought. The angel of death sounded awfully concerned considering she was already dead.

"Rinny, did you hear that?" The roaring in his ears had only just faded, and Matthew couldn't be certain, but he believed somebody was shouting at them from below.

She snuggled tighter against his solidity, loving the brush of his soft chest hair against her cheek. "Don't worry, it's just the angel of death coming to get me."

"But sweet, you're not dead."

Corinne lifted her head and saw Matthew's face swimming before her clearing vision. "I'm not?"

"No. We're alive and stuck in an elevator."

"You mean we get to do that again?" she asked, her eyes glowing.

"We do. Although I don't think now is the best time," he said, shifting a little as the elevator carpet began to chafe against his bottom.

"Wow! It felt like my whole body was coming undone. That's never happened to me before."

Smugness was not a trait Matthew would normally assign himself. But after a compliment like that it was hard to refrain. "I did try my best," he muttered.

"Just a few more minutes and we'll have you out of there!" a voice called to them from below.

This time they both heard it. Suddenly, it truly dawned on Matthew where they were. In the heat of things he'd forgotten how all of this had started. Quite clearly he remembered that it had begun when the elevator stopped.

"Matthew," a panicking Corinne whispered. "They're trying to get us out."

"Oh no." He sprung into action first, lifting Corinne off his body. Just then the elevator jerked back to life and Matthew could feel them descending. They had only seconds before the doors opened to the lobby and they were caught in a very compromising position.

"Here," he said as he tossed her panties back to her while at the same time trying to step into his pants.

Panic had long since set in, and it was making it that much harder for Corinne to dress. She managed to get her poet blouse and skirt on. But the bra was simply too much so she tossed it into the air, hoping it might up and vanish. The buttons on the blouse were also impossible to negotiate. Finally, she gripped the ends of the blouse and tied them together over her breasts praying that she wouldn't break any laws of indecent exposure when the doors opened.

She turned to Matthew and saw that his pants were on, but not buttoned. Just as he was pulling the green shirt over his head, the sound of the doors sliding open filled the tiny compartment.

A crowd of faces stood on the opposite side of the doors. Most of them curious rubber-neckers and a few hotel employees. A man in front wearing a tool belt and a concerned expression stepped forward. "Are you all right, ma'am? We heard you screaming and we all figured you were pretty frightened."

Matthew stepped out behind the doors with his hand still tucking in the strands of his shirt into his pants. Corinne saw suspicion in the handyman's face and quickly sought to cover up their liaison.

"I *was* scared," she lied.

This particular performance was going to take all of her talent. She had no time to prep the dialogue, her cheeks were assuredly on fire, and she could feel the ends of her blouse pulling free from the knot she had quickly tied. But the show must go on.

"You see, I hate elevators," she blurted out, sensing that she was digging herself a hole with no bottom, but unable to escape. "And when the doors closed and I heard that strange thunk, I lost it. Luckily, this man is a...is a...psychiatrist! And he was able to work me through my phobia."

"I worked her," Matthew concurred a little too enthusiastically.

A quick jab from her elbow to his ribs reminded him that this was her show.

A little bolder, a little more confident in her role as the entertainer, Corinne continued, "He started me off with a few breathing exercises..."

"Heavy breathing," Matthew interjected quietly behind her.

"Gradually moved me forward to the next stage of personal awareness. And finally, he was able to penetrate my subconscious to the very root of my fear."

"That's right," he repeated for the crowd. "Penetrated to the root."

Growling low under her breath, a warning sign to the heckler behind her that he would pay for his insolence, Corinne finished, "And, as a result, I don't think I will ever fear elevators again. In fact, I'm quite looking forward to my next trip."

The crowd, so taken with her story, actually applauded her success. She didn't have far to go to blush, so instead she did a small curtsey.

Behind her Matthew could barely contain his amusement. "I think we should probably get right back on that elevator. After all, we don't want all my good therapy to go to waste. Is it working now?"

The man in the tool belt nodded affirmatively.

Matthew took a step back and Corinne did likewise. The crowd started to disperse and together they breathed a sigh of relief that they had escaped disaster.

"That was close," Matthew muttered, although he knew he didn't have to tell Corinne.

"You're welcome," she said, smiling. When she saw the confusion in his eyes, she elaborated. "For my quick thinking and inventive story."

Matthew laughed outright. "Rinny, you don't think anyone actually believed that hogwash about the therapy?"

"And why not?" she asked, affronted. "I was very convincing."

"True," he admitted. "But the effect of the performance was spoiled by the fact that you've got your bra dangling from your skirt."

Corinne looked down to confirm his statement. And there it was. A near-transparent bit of lace hanging by a single hook on her skirt and betraying exactly what had went on in the elevator. Worse than that, it ruined a very good impromptu story. "Drat!"

Matthew laughed even harder. "Come on. Let's go upstairs to your room. No interruptions there, I promise."

Since she was more than ready for round two of...therapy, she was happy to oblige. Ripping the bra off her skirt, she tucked it inside the loose folds of her blouse and stepped back inside the elevator.

When she glanced up, however, the impossible stopped her breath. No, she thought. It couldn't be. Not here. Not now. But as the doors began to slide together the object of her astonishment turned and caught a glimpse of her between the two panels.

"Corinne!" he shouted. "It's me. Brendan."

"YOU PROMISE me you're not going to do anything so silly as fight over me." There was admonishment in her voice, but she couldn't completely mask her perverse thrill at the idea of two men fighting over her. It was, after all, terribly dramatic.

"I promise." Matthew had no intention of fighting the fool. Murder, on the other hand was not completely out of the question.

"All right. When the elevator stops, you know the drill. We're going to handle this in a calm and very adult manner." Corinne had pushed the top-floor button, purposely making the elevator ride all the way to the top before it started its descent. But the short ride wasn't nearly enough time to script the upcoming scene. Mostly, because she had no idea how she wanted to play this. "I'll simply tell Brendan we came to this island as friends."

Insistently, Matthew gripped both of Corinne's forearms and turned her to face him. "And then what?" he asked, his gaze intent on hers.

"I...I don't know."

"Not good enough, Rinny." He didn't mean to sound so harsh, but the rage he was feeling came in a distant second to the sense of hopelessness he felt at the idea of losing her to Brendan.

Immediately on the defensive, Corinne fired back. "I've made it very plain from the beginning how I felt about Brendan." Felt. Past tense. Even her own words betrayed her. Corinne sighed desperately. She was no better than anyone in her family. As fickle as the rest of them. Her traitorous heart couldn't decide which man it loved.

"What about how you feel about me?"

"Don't do this to me," Corinne pleaded. If he continued to push she might do something silly like tell him the truth about how she felt before she really knew what his own true feelings were. Despite her near certainty that he was in love with her, she needed proof that there was more to the emotion than just friendship and gratitude.

"We just made love. Doesn't that mean anything to you?" Matthew asked roughly.

"Yes. Of course it does, but you have to understand..."

"No, I don't. I don't have to understand anything. Hell, Rinny, I could have made you pregnant. Have you thought of that?"

"Ah-ha," she burst out.

"Ah-ha, what?"

She wasn't really sure. She only knew that she had just been utterly floored by the mere idea that she might be pregnant with Matthew's baby. Her heart was pounding so hard and her hands were shaking so much that she couldn't decide if what she was feeling was fear or joy. Finally, she said, "You did that on purpose!"

"You're damn right I did it on purpose," he confessed. "Understand this, Rinny. I'm tired of playing Mr. Nice Guy. I'm tired of biding my time waiting for you to wake up and realize what sort of man Brendan is."

"And what sort of man is he?" she asked defensively.

"Brendan is a twit and you know it. If you hadn't so stubbornly convinced yourself that you were in love with him you would see that."

Attacking Brendan was the wrong tactic. He could see that immediately. Rather than convincing Rinny she'd been wrong all this time, he had only added fuel to her defense system.

"Oh, I see," she returned loudly. "I haven't really been in love for almost a year with one man. Completely monogamous in my affections and utterly devoted to that person's happiness. No! I've just been stubborn! Thank you so much for pointing out what a fool I've been."

"I didn't say fool," he countered, knowing that he had wounded her pride. "I only meant to say that in your heart you know..." He stopped then, unable to finish that thought because in truth he didn't know how she felt.

"I know what?" she demanded.

Resigned to playing this out to its conclusion, Matthew held up his hands. "I guess only you know what you feel. All I ask is that you keep an open mind. And an open heart."

Suddenly sad, Corinne nodded in agreement. It seemed he'd been so close to telling her the right decision to make, but then he'd backed off. Maybe even he didn't know what the right decision was.

"Matthew, I need to know something."

She needed to know if what he felt for her was truly love or something less substantial. An emotion conceived while he was laid up in a hospital bed with only a few visitors to break up his day. Something so shallow, it could never withstand the test of time.

"Anything."

"Do you really lo..."

Her question was interrupted by the ding that signaled that they had reached their destination. The doors opened and Brendan was waiting for her. In a sweeping bear hug, he lifted Corinne off her feet and twirled her about.

Naturally, Rinny never saw the leggy blonde who walked off just after the doors opened. But Matthew did. It seemed Brendan was still acting true to form despite his impromptu appearance.

"Brendan, put me down," she said breathlessly, the air having been squeezed out of her lungs.

He dropped her rather unceremoniously and checked out his surroundings. "Nice place, babe. There's a casino downstairs. Maybe later you can head for the slots while I play a few hands of poker. I wouldn't mind taking some of these tourists for a few bucks."

"Sure," Corinne muttered, not really listening to what he was saying. Her mind was too focused on the fact that Matthew was stepping behind her. The heavy weight of his hand rested on her shoulder.

"Relic!" Brendan announced. "I heard you were here. There was some kind of bet going on at the office. Something about you taking a vacation, I think. Not too sure. So what brings you down here?" he questioned good-naturedly.

"Uh...uh..." Corinne stuttered over her ready excuse. She just couldn't seem to think.

"I wanted to go to an island for vacation," Matthew replied casually.

"How about that, you and Corinne picking the same place. Small world."

"Not really," Matthew muttered under his breath.

Corinne heard his mutterings and joined the conversation before things got out of hand. "Are you staying at the hotel then?"

Brendan looked confused. Not a unique expression, Matthew noted.

"Babe, I came all this way to be with you. You know, win you back. Pretty romantic, huh?"

Actually it was the most effort he had ever extended on her behalf. She was about to comment on that when he said, "And if I can get a great tan at the same time, then that's just icing on the cake."

Suddenly tired, Corinne just wanted to go back to her room and think about the day's events and what she was going to do next. To that end, she asked Brendan again, "Do you have a room at this hotel? Maybe we can meet for breakfast tomorrow morning?"

"Babe," Brendan said leaning in close, his brow arched in a way that implied he had other plans. "I figured I would be staying with you."

"Notachance," Matthew coughed into his fist.

"What was that, Relic?" Brendan queried.

"Nothing. He's allergic to sand," she offered. Fortunately, Brendan had his mind on other things, namely getting her into bed, so he didn't realize the ridiculousness of her statement. "The truth is, I've gotten a little too much sun today. I was on my way up to bed when you arrived. I really don't think I could let you stay with me. Perhaps you can get a room."

"But, babe?" Brendan began, and then let the sentence stand as if those two words were enough to convey his disappointment and his astonishment at being denied.

Satisfied that she had no intention of letting Brendan stay with her, Matthew was willing to be magnanimous. "You can stay with me, Brendan. I've got two double beds. And as long as you don't snore, it's yours."

It was also a perfect way to keep his eye on the man. If he tried to get to Rinny, Matthew would know about it and stop it. And if he followed his traditional patterns and sought out other company for the night, he might just be able to arrange it so that Rinny caught her one true love in the act.

"You're all heart, Relic. Or should I say half heart." He laughed at his own joke.

Both Corinne and Matthew stared at a man who would make a joke about a near-death experience. Matthew wanted to turn to Rinny and say, "See!" But instead he just turned and headed back for the elevator.

"I left my bag at the front desk," Brendan informed them. "I'll get it real quick."

Corinne watched while he jogged off to the front desk. He stopped, picked up his bag, and flirted with the girl behind the counter. Shaking her head, she joined Matthew in the elevator. He stood holding the door open button, but said nothing.

"It was awfully nice of you to let Brendan stay with you," she said conversationally.

"Nice had nothing to do with it. I wanted to keep my eye on him. Having him underfoot seemed the best way to accomplish that."

"Oh."

"Okay," Brendan announced as he approached the elevator. "I'm all set."

"Did you get that girl's number?" Matthew asked casually.

"No, they don't have numbers here at the hotel. Just extensions," he answered before he realized that Corinne, the woman he was supposed to be winning back, was in the elevator with him. "Not that I would ever call that girl. I've decided to make a commitment to you, babe. You're my one and only." He put an arm around her shoulders and hugged her tight.

Corinne smiled limply. The elevator jumped to life and the three rode up in silence. To say she felt awkward standing on the very spot where she had made love with one man while the man who was supposed to be her one and only love draped himself over her shoulders, was an understatement. Heat filled her cheeks, and she wondered how close she was to just throwing back her head and howling at the injustice of it all.

She'd been so dedicated to Brendan. Always careful not to let her eyes or her heart wander as other members of her family had done so often in the past. All this time she had convinced herself that Brendan was her fate. Her destiny. Her future. Now that future was a blur. Filled with vague images of Matthew...bouncing a little baby boy on his knee.

A baby, she thought shakily. She couldn't have a baby! The first rule of acting was never ever to do a scene with an animal or a baby! They always stole the show. That, and they got to wear cuter outfits.

Reigning in her irrational thoughts, Corinne tried to focus. What if she did decide that she'd been wrong to commit her heart to Brendan and chose to pursue a relationship with Matthew? How many months before her eye was turned again? How long before some other man came along and wooed her fickle heart? Was her true destiny to flit about from one relationship to the next never knowing the certainty or the permanence of true love?

Oh, the horrors of it all!

"Your floor, Rinny."

"Huh?" Her mind was still in a fog of what the future held in store for her.

Matthew gave her a gentle push to let her know it was her cue to get off the elevator. She stepped out into the hallway and tried desperately to remember if her room was to the left or the right.

"Hold the door a second for me, will ya, Relic?"

Stoically, Matthew stood by while Brendan stepped off the elevator and hauled Rinny up against his chest for a good-night kiss. His only consolation was that Rinny turned her head at the last second so all Brendan managed to kiss was her cheek. Maybe for the first time the veil was being lifted from her eyes and she was seeing Golden Boy for who he really was.

RINNY WOULD GIVE HIM one more second before she began to push him away physically. Her whole future was up for grabs, and she simply didn't have time for this. The fact that his lips weren't Matthew's lips, Matthew's gentle soft lips that had caressed her body so thoroughly earlier, didn't help. Then she felt Brendan's hand reach for her bottom. That was it. Corinne lifted her hands to his chest and pushed until he stumbled backward.

"Hey?"

"My sunburn," she explained weakly. "And Matthew is waiting."

With a shrug, Brendan left her and stepped back inside the lift. "Tomorrow then."

"Tomorrow," Corinne repeated.

"Tomorrow," Matthew reiterated ominously.

The doors closed and the two men were left to themselves. "I don't know what's gotten into Corinne. She's usually all over me."

Matthew said nothing.

"Hey, you don't think she met another guy, do ya?"

Honestly, Matthew replied, "No, she hasn't met anyone else."

"Then I don't get it," Brendan said finally. Then he seemed to get over his disappointment. "Oh well. 32601. 32601."

"What are you doing?"

"Just making sure I don't forget that extension the girl downstairs gave me earlier. 32601. It's an old trick I have. You repeat the number over and over. 32601. And then it sticks in your head for hours. 32601."

"I thought you were going to make a commitment to Corinne."

"I am," Brendan asserted. "That doesn't mean I can't make new friends though. You know, just to have someone to...play cards with."

Jackass, Matthew thought silently.

"32601. 32601."

"We're on the twenty-second floor," Matthew chimed in.

"Whatever. 32601. 32601."

"In room 22705, in case you get lost. Did you get that? 22705?"

"Yeah, okay," Brendan said, trying to concentrate. "22601. 22601."

Matthew could feel a sinister smile cross his lips. It

would have been fun to set him up and lead Rinny right to him. There would be no way for her to deny then that Brendan was never going to change.

But in the end he knew that would hurt her. And he just didn't have it in him to do that to her. So a little petty revenge would have to suffice.

"I've got a bottle of champagne in my room. Compliments of the hotel. You know I only ever drink beer. You should take it. I'm sure your friend will like it. You can drink it while you...play cards."

Brendan's face lit up. "Great idea, Relic! You know I used to think you didn't like me so much. But you're really all heart."

"No, no," Matthew corrected. "Half heart."

Brendan laughed at his own joke being used against him and Matthew chuckled along.

The fact that all of Matthew's teeth were showing didn't alarm Brendan as much as it should have.

9

SHE HAD TO KNOW if Matthew truly loved her.

It was that simple. As she lay on her bed staring at the ceiling contemplating the mysteries of love and life and listening to her face harden under a mask of green clay that was proven to enhance skin condition and reduce the fine lines that signify aging, that one realization came to her over and over again. If she could just verify that he really did love her then her choice was easy.

Of course, she would have to be equally honest with him. She would have to let him know that although currently her feelings were very strong for him that didn't mean they were permanent. After all, she had professed to love Brendan and look how easily she'd been swayed. One trip away from him with another man and...boom!

She was in love with someone else.

Well, at least no one could accuse her of not *trying* to carve out a different life for herself. But in the end she was a Weatherby. Fickle. Unfaithful. Flighty. All of her efforts for a normal life, a husband and children and happily ever after, wasted.

She considered calling her mother again for some motherly comfort and support. But her mother would never understand what Corinne was suffering. She loved the drama of multiple love affairs. She loved the attention of men, and the attention of the press when they found out about her newest man.

Corinne was honest enough with herself to admit that she didn't mind the attention she was currently receiving. After all, having two attractive men vie for her wasn't the worse thing that could happen to a girl. But nothing good could come of it. In the end she knew it would only lead to suffering.

This time she would hurt Brendan with her rejection.

Next time it would be Matthew. And that was simply untenable.

She just didn't see how it could be helped. The pattern was set. For almost a year she had claimed to love one man only to have another man seduce her and twist her heart to his side. Which meant all the rest was bound to follow.

All her previous pledges of no secret rendezvous with men that weren't her husband...gone. No having affairs that made the front of the tabloids...gone. No dramatic fights in the middle of the night that woke up the children...gone.

All the things that her parents had done to each other and that had made her feel ashamed and embarrassed for them were the very same things she was destined to repeat. Perhaps her face wouldn't grace the cover of the tabloids, she wasn't famous enough for that, but no doubt she would be the talk of the PTA.

Worse, she knew in advance the effect that her affairs would have on her children. She had wanted her children to grow up with the belief that their mother and father loved each other and only each other. Now, they were going to be left with the constant threat of divorce. They were going to experience the sinking sensation in the pit of their stomach when the fighting began, just as she had as a child. It wasn't fair.

Corinne placed a protective hand over her womb.

Was it possible that Matthew had gotten her pregnant? On their very first try? It seemed unlikely, but she wasn't stupid enough to think it was beyond the realm of possibility. Before, the thought of a baby had sent her into a tizzy. It still made her a little queasy. Maybe her particular family wouldn't be bothered by the idea of an unwed mother, but Corinne was old-fashioned enough to turn slightly red at the concept. And then there was getting fat, and not being able to dye her hair, and, of course, the actual pain of labor to consider. And when all that was done she would actually have to take care of it, which could mean hours and hours of lost beauty rest.

A baby.

With all of Matthew's good sense, good heart and forthright character. And all of her charm, wit, looks, flair, talent and gregariousness. A very even match. Perhaps it wouldn't be the worst thing in the world.

And it's not as though she would have to bear the stigma of unwed motherhood for long. No doubt as soon as Matthew learned that she was carrying his baby he would propose. It was just the sort of man he was. Brendan, on the other hand, would book a flight for Guam. That's just the sort of man he was.

A tiny kernel of an idea wormed its way into her head. It seemed when she really deliberated on the subject, Brendan turned out to be somewhat of a...jerk. A roving-eyed, shallow, inconsiderate, unromantic, self-absorbed...jerk. It wasn't that Corinne hadn't recognized these faults in the past, it was just that she had chosen to overlook them because of her devoted love.

She supposed the question she needed to ask herself was how she had ever fallen in love with him in the first place?

Knock. Knock.

Uh-oh. Corinne bolted out of bed and tied the terry-cloth robe tightly about her body. She had a suspicion that Brendan might try to wheedle his way into her bed despite her protests, but she was prepared for him.

The first thing Matthew saw when the door opened was green. He couldn't say for sure if the person standing in front of him was his Rinny or an alien replacement with green skin. The piles of red curls she wore on top of her head gave her away.

"Rinny, is that you?"

"Matthew!"

Perfect, she thought, disgusted with herself. The very last person she wanted to see her like this and she had just opened the door to him. It was too late to run to the bathroom to wash off the clay mask. Even if she could manage to get her hands on a washcloth, it wouldn't do her any good. When this stuff hardened, it turned into cement. As it was, she'd left it on too long and would probably need a jackhammer to get the gunk off.

Matthew stared hard at the green face that was actually starting to crack in some places. He believed she said his name, but since her lips weren't really moving behind the hardened mask, it was hard to be sure.

"What the hell is that?" he asked raising a finger to poke at the hardened clay.

"Itsforweenkles."

"Winkles?"

"Weeenkles," she shouted as much as the opening in the mask would allow.

"Oh, *wrinkles*," Matthew said, finally getting it. "You know you don't have to wear that stuff on your face. I don't mind that you have a few wrinkles."

"Room service!" The busboy had chosen that precise

moment to appear with a tray filled with what appeared to be a pot of tea and a healthy slice of cheesecake.

Fortunately for Corinne red cheeks couldn't be seen through the green gunk.

"Wouldyougetinhere," she mumbled, while pulling on Matthew's arm to indicate to him that he needed to come inside the room rather than blast her secrets about in the hotel hallway for anyone else to hear. She signed for the cheesecake and gave the busboy a generous tip. A payoff to keep the comment about the wrinkles to himself.

She closed the door and turned back to Matthew. "Fustoff, Idon'thaveweenkles."

"Huh?"

"Idon'thaveweenkles!"

"I told you I don't mind the wrinkles," he said again, eyeing the cheesecake and wondering how much of a piece she would miss. "Laugh lines on a woman's face are a sign of character."

"Ugggh!" Stomping off to the bathroom in a fury, she wet a washcloth and placed it over her face, loosening the mask. After a few minutes she was able to wash enough of the clay off so that at least she was able to speak coherently.

Matthew wasn't sure which was worse. A completely green face or a red face with green blotches. As long as he lived, he didn't think he would ever understand women. Most of them were a mystery, but Corinne took the cake.

"What I was trying to say," she enunciated as she wiped the goop from her face with the washcloth. "Is that I don't have wrinkles."

At least she'd better not have any wrinkles. She dashed into the bathroom and examined her face in the mirror. Perhaps there were a few slight, very slight, marks around her eyes. But Corinne would hardly call them laugh lines. More like chuckle creases. And surprisingly, the clay mask had done a remarkably fine job of firming up those creases.

"Rinny, are you all right?"

Once again, Corinne emerged from the bathroom. This time with a perfectly clean face. No need to discuss the creases with company.

"I just wore that stuff in case Brendan showed up at my door. One look at my appearance and he would get the idea that I'm not fit for company."

"I get it. Scare tactics."

"Exactly. Brendan has a hard time being in a room with anyone who isn't as attractive as he is, let alone taking that person to bed." Another fact that made her question how she could ever love someone like that in the first place. "Speaking of Brendan, how did you get out of the room without him asking you where you were going? You can't lie, but I doubt you would tell him you were coming down here to see me."

She was right. He wouldn't have been able to lie. Fortunately, he didn't have to when there was no one in the room to lie to. Brendan had already gone in search of the lucky inhabitant of 22601. Inwardly, Matthew chuckled. Still, he didn't want to hurt Rinny.

"He...uh...he was...uh...asleep! He was asleep," he repeated, a little more confident in his story.

Corinne just shook her head. "He's downstairs trying to pick up the girl who works behind the desk. That or he's succeeded in picking her up, and they are already heading back to her room. Like I said, you can't lie. And I know Brendan."

"Would it make you feel any better to know that I've

sent him on a wild-goose chase? And at this very moment, he might be offering a cheap bottle of champagne to a woman with a large husband who doesn't like poachers?"

It certainly made *him* feel better. Room number 22601 belonged to Bud, his poker friend, and his wife, Sally. There were two things in this world that Bud didn't like. Pretty boys and poachers. It was a particular discussion they had shared over a hand of poker.

"You didn't," Corinne accused, although she couldn't help but be pleased by his initiative and creativity.

"I did," he confessed willingly.

"Matthew, Brendan doesn't know how to protect himself. He's like a baby."

"Who is about to get spanked," Matthew added gleefully.

"This is serious," Corinne protested, although with a smile on her face at the suggestion that Brendan was currently facing an irate husband. "You should warn him."

"I will. Tomorrow. Right now I've got more important things on my mind." Matthew eyed the tray sitting in the middle of the room.

"Me, too." She sighed, turning away from him so she wouldn't have to confront him. "The thing is, I've been debating this over and over again in my head. Trying to decide what the best course of action is. What's best for me and for you."

"I only need a small piece, Rinny."

"But that's not right," Corinne told him. "You deserve more than just a piece. You deserve all of it. Everything I have to give. Anything less would be wrong."

"Really?" Matthew asked, excited by the thought.

"Yes."

"Great." Matthew walked over to the tray and picked up the cheesecake along with the matching fork. He perched himself on the bed and shrugged. "I figured the most I was going to get was half." He sunk the fork into the thick slice and popped the cake into his mouth.

Corinne considered making him eat that fork, but if she did that she wouldn't have anything left to finish off the cake with. Slowly she moved to stand before him. "I wasn't talking about the cheesecake," she said tightly.

"Uh-oh. You weren't?"

"No."

Matthew considered this. "Does this mean I have to give the rest back?"

"Yes." Regally, she held out her hand. Matthew placed the plate flat on her palm. Then she held out her other hand and Matthew turned over the fork.

Disappointed, but still savoring the one delicious bite he had managed to steal, he thought about what she might have been saying. "If you weren't talking about cheesecake, then what were you talking about?"

"About us!" she shouted. But she quickly calmed herself when she realized she was in danger of tipping over the cheesecake. Carefully, she returned the plate to the tray and spun about to face Matthew.

"I was trying to tell you that you deserve more than just part of my heart."

His face lacked expression, but Corinne could see the sudden turmoil building behind his eyes. A little shiver rippled down her spine. She supposed she was about to witness for the first time Matthew throwing a temper tantrum. It would be interesting to see how this might play out.

She'd never seen him enraged before. And an enraged man might be prone to confess things in the heat of passion. She hadn't prepared a script for this particular scene. Still, never let it be said that a Weatherby couldn't ad-lib when the situation called for it.

Standing, his arms crossed over his chest like a Viking, Matthew stated with finality, "That's good. Because I won't take part. I won't settle for half. It's got to be all or nothing."

"I knew it," she accused him, trying to shift blame from where it actually belonged. "I knew this would come down to an ultimatum."

"Ultimatum sounds like I'm offering you a choice. I'm not," Matthew railed. "I can't even believe you still think there is one to be made. Your true love is an idiot. Why is it that everyone else can see that but you!"

"Maybe because I'm an idiot, too! Have you ever considered that?"

"Yes," he responded rashly. "But then you talk stock investments and I know you are no dummy. I've doubled my profits from investments just in the last year!"

Dramatically, she gasped, as if an arrow had punctured her heart. Then, very carefully, she asked, "Are you trying to tell me you're only here for the money I can make for you?" Anything other than a *No, absolutely not,* answer was going to get him into serious trouble.

"Now you're being ridiculous," he told her, clearly getting frustrated with her intentional obtuseness.

"Oh, so first I'm a fool, now I'm ridiculous! For someone who pretends to care so much about me you certainly don't seem to have any trouble pointing out my flaws."

"Care about you?" Matthew repeated. The idea that she would use words so weak to express the havoc that was taking place in his heart only made him more infuriated. "Hell, woman, haven't you figured it out! I love you!"

Match, set, game. Or was it game, match, set? She always forgot. It hadn't been easy trying to lead him down that particular path what with having very little time to prepare her dialogue. Regardless, her mission was accomplished. Corinne had wanted to believe that he loved her, but she couldn't be sure until he said it.

After all, Matthew couldn't tell a lie.

However, that meant it was time to confess the unfortunate truth. "Fine!" Corinne roared back, just to keep up with the motif that they had created. "You want me, you got me. But just so you know, I can't make any promises about my fidelity."

It had been difficult enough imagining her with Brendan these past months. The thought of her with other men after she was his wife infuriated him no end. And it hurt him inside as nothing ever had. Defeated, Matthew slumped on the bed.

"Why would you cheat on me?"

His words cut her in two. Even the mention of her possible unfaithfulness was enough to cause him pain, which naturally brought about her own suffering. It was an impossible loop where no one won. Damn her parents for passing on such fickle genes. In an attempt to explain, Corinne joined him on the bed and wrapped an arm around his waist, loving the solid feel of his body next to hers.

"I have to tell you a story."

"Why do I get the impression this isn't going to be another fairy tale?"

Corinne sighed, then took a deep breath. "I was ten and I needed to bring in a current event for school. My parents always had lots of papers around the house.

Nothing newsworthy, of course. Such things were beyond them. But every Hollywood rag you could imagine cluttered our den. So I picked up this one paper, ripped off the front page and stuffed it into my notebook. In hindsight, I suppose I wasn't a very diligent student. I never really took the time to prepare my assignments. And this time it cost me big. I went into school that day and got up in front of the class to read my article. I just started reading it at first, not even really paying attention to what I was saying.

"The article began, That Damn Actress and her New Leading Man. Suffice to say, you've met my mother, and you know that her favorite word is..."

"Damn," Matthew said, more at the idea that Rinny had been exposed to her parents' infidelities at such a young age than for the sake of completing her sentence.

"The class laughed. They called my mom a cheater. I was so horrified. I went home and asked my mother if she was a cheater and she said she wasn't a cheater, she was a lover. And such a woman would never be content with just one man. But that was all right because my daddy was a lover, too, and he had many other women. It all seemed so backward.

"I knew right then that I didn't want to be a lover. That when I fell in love it would be forever. No affairs for me. No multiple marriages like my brother or multiple engagements like my sister. One man, forever. And if I lost him, well, then that was it for me."

"Rinny..."

"No. Let me finish. When I met Brendan, I'm not quite sure how it happened, but I decided he was the one. Which should have ended everything. Then you suggested the affair, which might have been okay if my feelings hadn't gotten in the way. Only now, I'm all mixed up. Clearly, I'm just like them. Which means that even though I have all these feelings for you, I can't trust them. Who knows what will happen the next time some new man enters my life?"

"You're not like them, Rinny." Matthew wrapped his own arms around her and pulled her close. "You're not a cheater."

"No, I'm a lover." She sighed sadly.

Matthew couldn't help but smile at her despondent admission. "Listen, I can't speak for your parents. I'm not much of a lover myself."

"No, that isn't true," she replied, immediately jumping to his defense. "You're a wonderful lover."

Blushing was such an unmanly thing, yet he couldn't seem to stop himself. "My point is that for two people who went through a bunch of different relationships your parents are still together. Maybe there is more love there than you think."

"But I don't understand how they could put the love they feel for each other aside, as though it means nothing. My brother was madly in love with his first wife, but then he ended up leaving her for someone else he was madly in love with. Then he did it again. And my sister swears she has loved all of her fiancés. I don't get it. It must be genetic."

"It has nothing to do with genetics," Matthew protested. "It's as simple as sometimes relationships don't work out. Sometimes feelings change and people go their separate ways. Sometimes people die and the ones left have to move forward. I can't promise what will happen to us over the years. No one can."

"Exactly! But if it's not true love, if you don't think we'll make it until the end, what's the point? A few months or years of great sex, ending in constant fighting and a bitter court battle fought between lawyers who don't even know us?"

Since Matthew had lost track of the conversation right after she said great sex, he figured the best course of action was to finish his point. "The point is, you don't know if it is going to be true love when you begin. True love takes time. I don't think anyone ever really recognizes it until the end. It has to stand the test of turmoil and joy. Sickness and health. And all that stuff."

"So you don't even know if I'm your true love?" she whined, inexplicably distraught at the notion that someday he might love someone else, too.

"I know I can't imagine my world without you," he reassured her. "I know that no one enjoys a Corinne Weatherby performance more than I do. I know that just the thought of your smile can make my day seem tolerable. And I know that when I was lying on the floor of that convenience store feeling my life slip away from me, my only regret was that I had never told you how much you meant to me. It didn't surprise me that yours was the first face I saw when I awoke from my coma. It seemed more like...fate. If that's not true love, then I can't imagine what is."

Wow! No one in Hollywood could have written it better. "You came up with all of that just like that? Off the top of your head?"

"From the bottom of my heart," he corrected her and mentally patted himself on the back for a fine play on words. Corinne wasn't the only one who could appreciate good drama.

Leaning forward she kissed his cheek. Then she leaned in closer and kissed the top of his head, then his other cheek, and finally she placed a soft chaste kiss on his mouth.

"What was that for?" he asked.

"A great script," she told him. Retreating a few inches, she shrugged her shoulders with uncertainty. "So what happens now?"

Matthew shrugged in return. "I guess that's up to you. I was wrong before. You do have a choice to make. But it's not a choice between Brendan or me. It's a choice between whether to take a risk or play it safe."

It didn't seem so much like a choice as it did a decision. She had to decide whether or not to forget the rules of love that she had set for herself so many years ago. But those guidelines for love that she had adopted at such an impressionable age seemed silly if they were going to prevent her the happiness that was right in front of her. Or beside her, depending on how you looked at it.

"It's a big decision you are asking me to make," she said.

"Maybe I can help," he offered and leaned in to really kiss her, something he'd been thinking about since the moment she'd opened the door.

Or at least since the moment she'd washed off all that green gunk.

Immediately, he felt her response. Her body went soft, her mouth opened to his silent command, and she returned his kiss with a passion that lit his gut on fire. Their tongues dueled for a time and the taste of her went to his head like whiskey. He remembered vividly how soft her skin had been under his hands and he wanted to feel it again. He reached inside her robe to find her naked underneath and nearly wept.

His hand found her breast and his fingers played with her nipple until it tightened under his touch.

"Matthew," she whispered as he bent his head to kiss

a trail from her mouth, down her neck, to the skin exposed by the gaping robe.

"Tell me you want me," he ordered her, needing to hear the words from her lips.

"I do want you. So much. I..."

His lips found her breast then, cutting off anything else she might have said. He sucked on her hard enough so that when he pulled his mouth away he could see the faint red mark left on her pure white skin. That mark, his mark on her body, was enough to make him howl with pleasure at the fact that this woman was his.

All his. No matter what she might say. He knew it. And he was pretty sure that she knew it, too.

His hand reached for her shoulder and he started to push her down onto the bed. A nice soft bed that would be worlds more comfortable than the elevator floor had been, if not quite as memorable. This time, he decided, he wanted to be on top.

But Corinne forestalled his efforts, bringing her hands up against his chest and pushing him away. "No, this is wrong," she protested even though she couldn't hide the desire that still flared to life in her eyes.

"Wrong?" How could that be when he had never felt anything more right in his life?

"Brendan is downstairs," she reminded him even as she covered herself with her robe.

"Yeah, I hope getting his face pounded. What's that got to do with us?"

"You're probably right. We probably do belong together..."

"There is no probably about it," he growled.

"Well, you're almost certainly right in suggesting that Brendan is only going to bring me pain. I know that. But that doesn't change the fact that I still have a relationship with him that has to end before I start something else. After all, he did come all this way just to see me."

"You're joking," Matthew exploded, not believing that she was still willing to stand by such a cretin. "He came all this way to *sleep* with you. That's it! And if I hadn't tricked him, he would be with another woman right now, with you only a few floors above him."

Corinne nodded slowly. "I know. I'm not making any excuses for him. But it's bad enough that I have to deal with the knowledge that I'm fickle. I won't be a cheater, too. Before he came down here it was easy enough to convince myself that any relationship we had was over. I could have an affair with you with a clean conscience. The fact that he flew down here after me proves otherwise. He still seems to think there is something between us. Regardless of what that 'something' means to him. So to be fair to all of us, I have to end it with him first."

Matthew wasn't sure which hurt more, the fact that she was right or the fact that he wasn't going to be getting any tonight.

Definitely, the fact that he wasn't getting any tonight.

However, it was clear that Rinny had issues she needed to address. Issues that her wayward parents had left with her. Matthew had met her mother. It didn't surprise him one bit that she might have in some way warped Rinny. The woman was strange, the way she cursed all the time.

But Rinny was working to overcome those issues. She had come pretty far in recognizing that Brendan was no good for her. That was huge. If she wanted to finalize the breakup, Matthew couldn't begrudge her that.

The truth was that he was absolutely delighted with the day's outcome.

Not only had he made love to her, but he'd also finally

told Rinny that he was in love with her. And although she hadn't said the same to him, and probably wouldn't until she ended it with Brendan, he now had faith that she did. She wouldn't have given herself to him the way she had if her heart hadn't been filled with love. Confident of the future, Matthew could walk away temporarily.

"Okay. You win. I'll go. But only if you promise that you'll end it with Golden Boy first thing tomorrow."

"First thing tomorrow," Corinne agreed. "I want this over with as quickly as possible. Once it is we'll talk about us."

"Us," Matthew said again. "I like the sound of that." He stood and walked to the door.

Corinne followed him and smiled as he slowly turned the knob on the door as if he was trying to cling to every extra second he had with her. Finally, he opened it and stepped out into the hallway.

"Are you going to put the green goo back on?"

Corinne chuckled at his accurate description. "I don't think that will be necessary. Brendan's probably had a rough night. I doubt he'll come looking for me."

Evilly, Matthew smirked. "Poor boy. I hope Bud took it easy on him."

"No, you don't."

"You're right, I don't," Matthew confessed gleefully. He leaned down and pecked her lips. "I'll see you right after first thing tomorrow. Good night."

"Good night."

Matthew stood back and let her close the door. Foolishly, he found himself hating the sound of the door closing. It seemed to sound so final.

He turned and headed back for the elevators, thinking that they'd only been separated by seconds and still he missed her. Shaking his head at himself, he concluded that he was becoming soft in his old age.

When he got back up to his room, Matthew wasn't at all surprised by the scene that greeted him.

Brendan was stretched out on one of the beds with an ice pack over his right eye and the gorgeous blond clerk cooing to him softly that everything would be all right.

"Rough night, Brendan?"

"Relic," Brendan greeted him. "You wouldn't believe what happened?"

"I might," Matthew uttered cryptically.

"I was looking for Monique," he began, tilting his chin in the direction of the woman still dressed in her hotel uniform. A uniform that was getting wrinkled in her devoted attention to the man on the bed. "And some other woman opened up the door. I realized I had the wrong room, but she was a nice lady and we had a few words. Then out of the blue this huge guy comes up behind her and starts accusing me of trying to make time with his wife. Can you imagine? Me?"

"Shocking," Matthew mocked.

"And then he decks me. Right in the eye. Good thing Monique found me or else he might have done permanent damage to my face."

"The horror."

"As it is, I don't know how I'm going to explain this black eye to Corinne."

"Or Monique for that matter."

Brendan had the decency to blush. "She's just a friend. Isn't that right, Monique? And you were just going, weren't you?"

"But I thought we..."

"...were going to play some bridge," Brendan filled

in. "I know. But not tonight, sugar. I'm beat. This has been a traumatic experience."

Monique stood, and a sour expression graced her countenance that made her look very unattractive. Matthew didn't think he would ever understand Brendan's tendency to roam when he had someone who looked like Rinny. But it was too late now. Rinny was his.

Monique stormed out and slammed the door behind her.

"Pretty huffy," Matthew commented.

"She's just sore about missing out on our game of bridge."

"You play bridge with four people."

"Whatever," Brendan shrugged. Then he said philosophically, "I guess it's all for the best anyway."

"Why do you say that?"

"I came down here to make a commitment to Corinne. I guess that means I should probably stop playing...cards with anyone else."

Matthew felt his chest tighten. "I don't get you. Why would you want to make a commitment to anyone when you know you can't live up to it?"

"That's what I say!" Brendan concurred, seemingly unaffected by Matthew's insult. "But Corinne thinks I'll be different once I'm married. She thinks that I have the capacity for great emotion," he quoted.

Matthew knew damn well that Brendan didn't even know what he was saying. But that he was saying it made him nervous.

"What do you mean married? Are you here to propose to Rinny?"

Brendan dug his hand into the front pocket of his designer jeans. He pulled out a small box that looked suspiciously as if it came from a jeweler. He popped it open and Matthew felt the air leave his lungs.

Settled inside, on a mound of blue velvet, was a one-carat solitaire diamond ring.

"Do you think she'll like it?"

Unfortunately, he did. He was deathly afraid she might like it too much.

10

"I DON'T KNOW what to say." Corinne stared down at the box in Brendan's hands.

Why now? How could this possibly be happening after I already decided to break up with you? Why would the fates play such a mean and nasty trick by presenting me with this ring, but having the wrong person attached to it?

In fact, Corinne could actually think of a great deal of things to say. She just couldn't say them out loud to Brendan. For the first time in her life she was speechless.

The two stood together on the white sand beach facing the ocean and the early-morning sun. He'd come for her before breakfast and had asked if they could take a walk along the beach. A perfect setting for a breakup, Corinne decided.

She had scripted the entire scene in her head last night. Right down to the part where he cried and begged her to take him back, but she tearfully refused because of her feelings for another man. Purposefully, she had worn her sea-green sleeveless sundress, as she knew that the pale-green color would best highlight her red eyes when the tears started to flow.

In her mind the whole scene was going to be wonderfully, tragically dramatic.

That was until Brendan reached into his front jean pocket and pulled out the most spectacular ring she had ever seen. A ring for her. The one thing she had wanted most in this world for the past year from the person she had wanted it from for a year...minus one day. It was all so surreal. All her dialogue went flying right out of her head and she was left stranded with nothing to say.

The sound of some children running for the water broke her daze. She watched while a sister and a brother splashed about in the water and their mother called to them not to go too far out. The children waved to their mother and continued with their game of who could stay under the water the longest.

The family scene struck a deep chord in Corinne's heart. This was what she wanted for herself. A family. A loving husband who would be there for her, forever. Laughing children she would scold when they got themselves into water that was too deep.

That opportunity stood right in front of her holding a box. The sun blinked over the diamond in his hand as if to mock her.

Take me. The ring called to her. *Grab me and put me on your finger and live out the dream. You and Brendan, forever.*

It was so tempting her fingers almost itched. She had to hold them against her body to keep them from twitching.

"It is a beautiful ring," she noted, almost as if in a trance caused by the dazzling shiny rock.

"Nothing but the best for you, babe."

Corinne glanced up at Brendan. There were definitely a few pros to consider if she took the ring. If she married Brendan she would be holding firm to her belief that there was only one true love for everyone. Maybe she had been right all along to think that he was the one for her. Maybe it was her feelings for Matthew that were the anomaly.

The cons, however, quickly followed.

Corinne knew that the idea of her and Brendan forever was totally unrealistic. He'd cheated on her too many times in the past for him to change his ways overnight. She'd been naive to think that a ring on his finger could change the man he was.

He was insensitive, immature and shallow. In fact, when she got right down to it, the only reason for accepting his offer would be so that she could stubbornly cling to her idea that there was only one true love.

That and she would get to keep a big diamond ring!

But the biggest con of all, the only one that really mattered, was that she was in love with Matthew. He was no anomaly. He was the real thing. And she knew it. It was impossible to say where their relationship would go from here, but it was also impossible to accept someone's ring when she was in love with somebody else.

"Well, babe? What's your answer?"

"You know, since I've known you, I don't think you have ever called me by my real name."

"Sure I have, babe. I do it all the time. So what's your answer? You going to make an honest man out of me?" he asked charmingly.

An impossible task to be sure. "Where did you get that black eye?"

Caught off guard, he stuttered for a few seconds then answered, "You wouldn't believe it. This door was stuck and I was pulling on it and...bam, the doorknob caught me right in the eye."

Corinne considered asking him why he was on his knees trying to open a door, but didn't bother. She knew he was lying and that was all that mattered. It made her answer that much easier. "The truth is, Brendan, I can't..."

"Stop!"

The couple turned their head in the direction of the shout. Matthew was racing toward them, his expression grim. Out of breath, his weak lung aching, he said, "You can't do this, Rinny."

"Matthew, I was just about to..."

"I know what you were just about to do and I won't let you do it. I don't care how pretty the damn ring is."

Her temper immediately burst into life. How dare he suggest she was going to take the ring after she had told him that she had already made up her mind to break up with Brendan! After she had confessed to him the only real reason why she had stayed with Brendan in the first place.

"What's this all about, Relic?" Brendan questioned.

"It's about the fact that you're a jerk, and I won't let Rinny marry you."

"You won't *let* me?" Corinne repeated, sure that she must not have heard him properly.

"That's right," Matthew argued, sticking to his guns although he feared they weren't fully loaded. "You know it would be the biggest mistake of your life."

"Did he just call me a jerk?" Brendan asked of no one in particular.

Corinne wasn't paying any attention to Brendan. Her focus was on Matthew. "Maybe it would be, but it would be my mistake. You can't tell me what to do just because you love me, Matthew."

"Wait a minute!" Brendan shouted. "You love her?"

"I thought I did," Matthew replied. "But I couldn't love anyone so thick-headed as to marry a man like you."

Corinne gasped with outrage at the verbal arrow that pierced her heart and took several steps back to get her bearings. This was a Matthew she had never seen before.

Gone was his easygoing demeanor and inherent politeness. If she searched his pockets, she doubted she would find any tissues on him this day. In his place was a tiger. An animal engaging in battle for his mate.

Actually, when she thought of it like that, his possessiveness didn't seem so bad. In fact it was really quite romantic.

"Was that a shot at me?" Brendan asked.

Matthew glared at the buffoon. It was a horrible thing to be involved in a fight with a man who didn't even get it when you were insulting him.

"Because I think it was. And I also think you called me a jerk."

This was probably the point where Matthew should apologize for his behavior. After all, it wasn't Brendan's fault that Corinne thought she was in love with him. Really, he was just a bystander. But that wasn't the mood Matthew was in today. Today, he was a wild man fighting for his future. And if Brendan was an innocent party who happened to get caught in the crossfire, well...

Tough! Matthew shoved Brendan's shoulder forcing him to take a step back. "Yeah, it was a shot at you, you jerk. What are you going to do about it, Golden Boy?"

"And another thing. I don't like you calling me Golden Boy," Brendan retaliated with a shove of his own.

Corinne closed her eyes. It was one thing to fantasize about two men fighting over her; it was a totally different thing to live it. She was about to step between the two overgrown children when a little girl's shout for help caught her attention.

"Help. My brother!"

Corinne scanned the water and saw the girl pulling herself onto the sand. She raced to grab her and helped carry her farther onto the shore. "My brother," the girl cried. "He went under the water and I can't find him."

Instantly, Corinne turned her gaze to the clear water. It was as smooth as glass. Not a ripple. Then she saw it, a small hand coming out of the water, breaking the surface then receding under the water once again.

Without a thought in her head, she raced into the water until she was hip deep. Just a few more steps and she would be precisely where she had seen the boy's hand. But suddenly the ocean floor gave out beneath her.

One second she was waist deep in water, then the next she was stepping off what felt like a ledge and suddenly she completely submerged.

Instantly, panic set in as she tried to scramble her way to get her head above the water.

"Help!" she screamed as loudly as she could. But the water quickly filled her mouth, as she was unable to keep her head above the water by using her legs.

Instead Corinne went under again and this time she let herself sink to the bottom so she could use the ocean floor to bounce off of and propel her back to the top. When she opened her eyes, she saw the little boy floating in front of her. His eyes were closed.

Desperate, she grabbed hold of him and with all of her strength bounced off the bottom. As soon as she felt her face break the surface of the water, she screamed again, a garbled, "Help!"

But before she could refill her lungs with oxygen, she was once again sinking back under the water. The pressure to breathe was a horrible pain in her chest. She knew she couldn't last much longer. Every instinct she possessed was telling her to open her mouth and breathe, but she knew she would only end up swallowing water.

Then all of a sudden, seemingly out of nowhere, there were hands around her shoulders. She was being lifted to the top, both she and the boy she still carried. As soon as she broke the surface, she sucked in air. Her next thought was to make sure the boy's head was above water as well. She couldn't be sure whether or not he was breathing, but at least his mouth and nose were above the water.

The hands that had pulled her out of the water dragged her onto the beach. Immediately she collapsed, her legs unable to support her. Coughing and spitting out the water that she had taken in, she wasn't aware of what was happening, but she felt a crush of people move in on her.

"The boy," she coughed. "The boy!"

"He's breathing," she heard one voice say. "Let's get him back to the hotel."

Corinne closed her eyes in relief.

Lying next to her, Matthew struggled to take in air. The race into the water, the exertion of pulling Corinne and the boy out, then the use of any air he had left to administer CPR to the child, had robbed him of all of his oxygen. His lungs simply weren't strong enough to handle this type of crisis and he fell back into the sand gasping for air as he struggled to regain his breath.

Brendan, however, who had only come to his aid in time to pull Corinne onto the sand, was fine and kneeling over Corinne's collapsed body.

Which was why he was the first person she saw when she opened her eyes.

"Brendan," she croaked, her voice hoarse from all her coughing.

"I'm here, babe. I'm right here. You're going to be fine."

"Brendan." She sighed. "You saved my life?"

On his back in the sand, a few feet away from her, Matthew heard what he thought was a statement and shut his eyes in resignation. It was over. Brendan had offered her a ring and now she believed he was responsible for saving her life. If he tried to suggest otherwise, he would only sound petty. Besides, it didn't matter. Rinny was okay. She was alive and that was all that counted. He should be grateful.

So why was he so sad?

Then a rush of medical people surrounded Corinne as she tried to sit up. "Are you all right, miss?"

Dazedly, Corinne nodded. Everything was still such a blur. "I shouldn't have gone in after him. I forgot I don't know how to swim. I should have called for help. Is he all right?"

"He's going to be fine, miss," the medic assured her. "Let's get you to the hotel infirmary. We just want to check you out and make sure you're all right."

She felt herself being lifted and when she raised her head it was Brendan's face she saw. After a few steps she finally was able to find her voice again. "Where's Matthew?"

But he wouldn't answer her, and she was too weak to say anything else. The adrenaline that the near drowning had stirred to life finally subsided from her system and she found herself impossibly tired. Unable to hold her head up, she let it drop against Brendan's shoulder and let the darkness overcome her.

HER WINDOW. Her dresser filled with her accessories. Her double bed. It was her room in the hotel. That's where she was. It had taken several minutes after she had first opened her eyes to assimilate to her surroundings. But now it was all coming back. The proposal, then her and Matthew fighting, then Brendan and Matthew fighting, then the little girl calling for help, and the boy in the water and the awful certainty that she was going to drown.

Vaguely, she recalled the feel of someone pulling her from the water. After that she remembered seeing Brendan's face swimming above hers as she lay in the sand.

"Brendan?"

"I'm right here, babe."

He was seated in a chair next to her bed. As soon as he heard his name he gripped her hand in his. It was probably the most caring gesture he had ever shown her.

"How long have I been asleep?"

"A few hours. The nurse said it was okay to let you sleep though. Sometimes that's what happens after a near-death experience. Your body gives out and you need a few hours to recharge your batteries. How do you feel?"

"Fine," she said. It was the truth. Her throat was a little sore. And her ribs hurt a bit, but aside from that she knew she was perfectly healthy. "Where's Matthew?"

A knock at the door distracted Brendan. He got up to open it and Corinne found herself disappointed at the sight of the woman who entered the room. She had hoped it would be Matthew.

"So how is my patient?" The large Bahamian woman asked. She wore a white uniform and a nurse's cap so there was no mistaking who she was. Her island accent was thick, but Corinne had no problem understanding her. She had a gentle face and Corinne knew that the little boy was in good hands.

"I'm fine. But the boy?"

"Oh, he's going to be okay. His parents took him to

the hospital to have him checked out, but I know he's going to be just fine. He wasn't in the water too long, and the man who saved you both knew CPR. He got the boy back to breathing right away."

The man who saved her. Corinne tried to recall the event, but everything was such a blur. Brendan had been leaning over her when she'd opened her eyes. His was the first face she had seen, so she had assumed that he was the one who had rescued her.

"I didn't know you knew CPR."

Brendan appeared confused. "I don't, babe."

The nurse corrected Corinne's mistake. "Oh, he wasn't the one who saved you, child. It was that other man. The big one. He pulled you and the boy out of the water, then gave the boy the CPR. That man was a real hero."

The nurse didn't have to say any more. Corinne knew only one hero. The same man that pulled her and the little boy out of the water was the same man who tried to stop a burglar from robbing a convenience mart. The same man she loved with all of her heart.

"Brendan, where is Matthew?"

"He's gone."

"Gone?"

"Yeah, it was really weird. He came in to see how you were doing, told me to take good care of you, and then he left. He had his bags with him. It looked like he was taking off for good."

Corinne was confused. She didn't understand why he would leave. No, that wasn't true. The scene before the accident came back to her in a rush of memory as well as Matthew's words. He thought she was going to take the ring. He thought she was going to marry Brendan despite what had happened between them.

The fool!

Then again, she supposed she couldn't blame him. For the past week she'd done nothing but go on about how Brendan was her one true love. She guessed she could understand why he might believe that she would choose Brendan over him. After all, she'd been foolish enough to fall in love with him in the first place. Or had she?

"I've got to go," Corinne announced. She rolled out of bed and wobbled a bit as her feet hit the floor.

"You can't go, babe, you're still shaky."

Not shaky enough to stop her from going after Matthew, she determined. Corinne started to wander about the room gathering her belongings. She pulled out the suitcases she had stored under the bed, opened them, and began carelessly to toss her things inside. For the first time in her life she cursed all of her clothes.

"You don't get it, Brendan," she explained. "I have to go after him. He thinks I'm going to marry you. I've got to stop him before he does something stupid."

Like quit his job or move to another country or—horror of all horrors—forget that he ever loved her in the first place.

"Nurse, tell her she shouldn't leave," Brendan asked the older woman.

But the woman just laughed and shook her head. "I don't think there is anything I could say that would stop this woman from going after the man she loves. Just take it easy, child." With those words of advice, she left the room.

"But I'm the one you love. Right? You wanted to marry me. I bought a ring. I'm going to settle down. Aren't I?" Brendan asked, clearly confused by everything that had happened.

That brought Corinne up short. Frustrated to have to

take precious minutes away from her packing, she stood before Brendan. "What's my name? Quick!"

"Uh...uh...Corinne. I know your name, babe."

"Yes, but it took you a few seconds before it came to you, didn't it? What's my favorite movie?"

"This one is easy. Any movie your mother is in."

"Wrong! I hate my mother's movies. *When Harry Met Sally* is my favorite movie. The movie about two friends who loved each other the whole time, but it took them twelve years to realize it...." Corinne stopped talking as her words played back in her head.

"I can't believe it." She slapped her forehead as the realization of her true feelings dawned on her for the first time. "What a fool I've been! It's all so clear. I never loved you!"

"You didn't? But what about all that stuff about forever and ever, and I was your soul mate and you were my destiny?"

"Wrong. All of it wrong. Because what I felt for you is nothing compared to what I feel for Matthew. I love his patience, his sturdiness and his dependability. I love his romantic streak, his lovemaking, his dancing. That's what true love is. It's friendship. And caring. And being there for one another even when times are bad."

"I can be there when times are bad. Wasn't I there on the beach today?"

Corinne studied him. "Really? Let me ask you this. What would you do if I threw up on your shoes?"

"Oh gross!"

"My point exactly. I'm sorry to have to be so blunt about this. It was my intention to break this to you gently. But somehow I think you will survive."

"I will?" Brendan asked dully. "But you said that you

were the only woman who would ever really love me. So if you never really loved me..."

The situation was about to become uncomfortable. She truly didn't want to hurt Brendan. But she also didn't have time to hold his hand. She had a man to catch. Then Corinne had a brainstorm.

"Let me put it to you like this, Brendan. With me out of the picture, you're free to chase any woman you want with no recriminations and no more nagging from me. The clerk downstairs. Marjorie from human resources. Or some woman you haven't even met yet. Any woman you want."

"Any woman I want?"

"All the fish in the sea," Corinne reiterated.

"What do fish have to do with anything?"

Corinne sighed. "Brendan?"

"Yes."

"Go find yourself a nice girl."

He shrugged his shoulders and turned to the door, but then he paused. "I'm really allowed?"

"Absolutely," she assured him.

"Cool," he muttered on his way out.

Already forgotten, she knew, Corinne turned back to her packing. She didn't know why, but she felt this rush of urgency and the instinct that if she didn't find Matthew and tell him that she loved him soon all would be lost.

Of course that could just be her dramatic streak running amuck.

But she didn't think so.

WELL, it was done.

Matthew had just finished the last sentence of his resignation letter and was currently sending it to the printer.

He hated to do it. He loved this company. He loved the work and he loved the people he worked with. Unfortunately, that was the problem. During the flight back to New Jersey, he had weighed the options in his mind and decided that his only course of action was to resign.

He worked too closely with Corinne. To meet with her, discuss the economic forecasts with her, eat his bologna and cheese sandwich with her every day, knowing that she was married to a buffoon, was too much for any man to handle. Certainly too much for him.

But that was an excuse and he knew it.

The truth was he couldn't do all those things with her not because of her marriage to Brendan, but because of his own broken heart. It would eat at him day in and day out being close to her, but not being able to kiss her or to hold her. Things would be awkward.

He had promised her once that when the affair was over they would be able to go back to being friends, and he hated to break that promise. But he knew that when he had made it, he had been supremely confident that he would be able to change her mind as well as her heart.

The fact that he hadn't was a two-pronged pain— knowing that he was going to have to live the rest of his days without her and knowing that he hadn't been able to spare her from the heartbreak that being married to Brendan would eventually cause. The man would never be faithful to one woman, and Matthew couldn't stand by and watch that happen.

He sighed deeply and stood up. He left his office and started the long walk down the hall to the printer that held his uncertain future in its outgoing bin. He took his steps carefully, slowly, as one who was on a death march might take. He couldn't shake the feeling that he was an inmate on death row, and it wasn't a printer waiting for him at the end of this long march, but a large chair with lots of wires attached to it.

Maybe Rinny was right all along. Maybe there was only one true love for every person. And when you lost that love you were lost as well. Matthew had enough sense to know that eventually he would recover from this, but right now he felt as though someone had put an abrupt end to all his dreams. And for the life of him, he couldn't imagine ever feeling about another woman the way he felt about his Rinny.

He reached the printer and extracted the letter from the bin. It was all rather vague. Due to personal issues he could no longer continue to work for this company. No doubt the president would try to talk him out of it, but he was resolute. It was going to be hard enough even to see Rinny again, let alone work with her.

Already, he was cringing at the scene that he knew would take place upon her return. All the women in the office would gather around to ooh and ah over her ring. All of them would talk of bridesmaids, who would be chosen, who would be left out.

And worse would be the guys in the office chucking Brendan on the shoulder and offering words of condolence and telling him to escape now while he still had the chance. No doubt Brendan would laugh and make stupid comments about how he had to do it, and about how the ball and chain that was attached to his ankle would really chafe his skin.

The jerk.

"You!"

The shout echoed down the hallway and caused several of the customer service reps tucked away in their cubicles to poke their heads out into the hallway.

Matthew raised his eyes and was more than surprised to find Rinny standing at the end of the long hallway. Her red hair was flying about her, her arm was stretched out, and her finger was pointing directly at him.

She wore jeans and one of those loud floral Hawaiian shirts she had tried but failed to talk him into buying, so it was apparent that she wasn't here to work. Which meant she had come into the office for some other reason.

He noted that the hand she was currently pointing at him was her left hand. He strained his eyes to see the gleam of a diamond shining from it, but could not. A burst of hope exploded inside his chest. Was it possible that she had turned down Brendan's offer of marriage?

"Me, what?" Matthew asked, raising his voice so that it carried down the long corridor. Matthew could see that the heads that had poked out of their cubicles turned in unison toward Corinne.

"You left in the middle of a fight!" she accused him.

The office workers turned back to look at him.

"You were going to accept Brendan's engagement ring!" he shouted back.

There was a chorus of gasps from the spectators at this unexpected news.

"Ah-ha!" Corinne fired back.

"Ah-ha what?" Matthew wanted to know. He couldn't stop the smile that he knew was forming on his lips. Inside, he was almost giddy. She wouldn't be here if she had accepted Brendan's proposal.

"That is the reason we were fighting. You didn't trust me to do the right thing. You didn't trust me to know my own heart!"

It was true. He had jumped to the conclusion that she would accept Brendan's proposal even though she had told him she was going to break up with him. But it was a logical assumption to make. The ring had been really big.

"I thought he was your one true love," Matthew charged.

All heads turned back to Corinne. "That's impossible. He can't be my one true love. Especially because I never really loved him."

There was another chorus of oh-mys from the crowd.

Matthew smiled broadly. So wide he was sure Corinne could see it. He took a few steps in her direction "So if *he's* not your one true love, then who is?"

Corinne, too, walked toward him, a deliberate sway in her hips. It was time to end this particular play once and for all.

"You," she answered him boldly. "You are my one true love. I was just too blind to see it."

A few more steps from him and a few more steps from her and suddenly she was running toward him and Matthew was sweeping her up into his arms. The women in the office sighed longingly, and a few of the men snickered. But everybody was pleased with the performance.

"I love you," he whispered against her throat, trying to reach everywhere with his lips.

"I love you, too. I think I always have. I just needed you to tell me what was already in my heart." She kissed him back and once more felt the pure joy of the moment. "You're the only one who has ever seen the real me and still loved me."

"And I love the real you. You never have to dye your hair, or wear green contact lenses, or put on a push-up bra again!" he proclaimed. He hugged her tightly against his body. Lifted her, and swung her about.

Although Corinne was caught up in the moment, she could still hear the staggered remarks from the audience.

"She dyes her hair?" one woman asked.

"And wears colored contact lenses?" another repeated.

"Forget that," another said. "She wears a push-up bra. That's how she does it!"

Corinne pulled her head back and looked into her one true love's eyes. Her smile was huge, but her teeth were clenched. "You just told everybody I work with I wear a push-up bra. You're going to pay for that."

Matthew hoped so. He hoped he would spend the rest of his life paying for it. As long as Corinne was a part of that life, he would accept his punishment with glee.

After all, he had found his one true love.

_____Epilogue_____

IT HAS BEEN SAID that a bride is the producer, the director and the star of the greatest production ever performed in that woman's life—her wedding.

Corinne took this particular idiom to heart. She just hadn't counted on her mother not exactly following the script.

"I just don't understand. Why him, damn it? Why him?"

Grace Weatherby sat on a stool in the back room of the tiny chapel where the ladies were making their final preparations before the curtain went up. She dabbed at her damp eyes with a handkerchief, careful not to smudge her mascara, while she watched Darla and her daughter, Myra, fuss with the train on Corinne's exquisite gown.

"I think he's cute," Myra stated.

Corinne looked down at her perfectly coiffed and mind-numbingly beautiful sister. She had purposefully gone with lavender for the bridesmaid's dresses knowing it was Myra's worst color. She had absolutely no intention of being upstaged for this particular performance.

"You stay away from him," she said. She wagged a finger at her sister in an effort to be funny, but the real threat in her voice was anything but humorous.

Myra just smiled and shrugged her shoulders.

"Don't worry about her," Darla whispered into her friend's ear as she fluffed the back of her veil. "He only has eyes for you."

It was true, Corinne thought. Not only did he love her, but he also thought she was the most beautiful woman in the world. She just wanted to keep it that way, so the least amount of exposure he had to Myra, the better.

"It's just that he's so...so...so entirely unassuming," her mother continued to complain. "He's nothing like your brother. Certainly nothing like your damn father."

Exactly, Corinne thought. Matthew wouldn't flirt with other women. He wouldn't always try to steal the scene from her. And as a bonus, he would never again reveal any more of her secrets to an audience.

He had promised.

"I love him, Mother. That's all you need to know."

"If you insist." She sighed. "And are you still planning on living...here? In this damn state?"

"This is where we work, Mother. Matthew and I are perfectly happy here."

"I'll never understand you. How is it possible that you are a Weatherby?"

Smiling, Corinne informed her mother. "You don't have to worry, Mother. After tonight I'll no longer be a Weatherby. Instead I will be a Relic...oooh."

"Yikes," Myra gasped.

"Awful," her mother groaned.

Corinne repeated the name again to herself silently. *Relic. Corinne Relic. Rinny Relic.* Heaven forbid!

"How about Corinne Weatherby-Relic?"

"Better," her sister said.

"Not entirely awful," her mother allowed. "Although it will never fit on a marquee."

Darla stared at the three women wondering what all

the fuss was about. She thought *Corinne Relic* had a nice ring to it. But then again, she could be biased considering that she'd won over a hundred dollars betting on her favorite couple.

"Myra, don't slouch," Grace said as she stood, her gray silk dress falling about her svelte frame without a wrinkle. "Everyone is going to be looking at you. You have a reputation you need to uphold for your fans…even in damn New Jersey."

Corinne frowned at the thought of everyone looking at Myra, but her sister just winked at her.

"I don't think they'll be looking at me today, Mother. Corinne's got a lock on this particular scene."

Mouthing a silent thank you, Corinne turned toward the door that had just opened. Her impossibly debonair father stepped inside, looking exceptional in his tuxedo and top hat.

"There's my girl."

"Hi, Daddy. Is Matthew waiting for me?"

"He is. Looks as nervous as your brother did his first opening night. I'm rather afraid he might lose his lunch, if you know what I mean."

Unfortunately, she did. And since they both sort of had bad luck in that particular area, Corinne crossed her fingers and prayed that Matthew would make it through the ceremony.

Nothing could go wrong. She wouldn't allow it. This was going to be the first and last production staring Corinne Weatherby as the bride and she insisted that it be perfect. Nothing was left to chance. No detail was unimportant. Everything from the handkerchief in Matthew's pocket to the altar boy's shoe choice was accounted for.

The flowers were shades of pink and purple that perfectly matched the bridesmaids' gowns. The woman singing in the church was a personal friend of her brother's, who, as luck would have it, also happened to be a major Broadway star.

Corinne's hair, her makeup, her nails, had been done by Hollywood's best. Her mother had insisted. And her gown and veil were done by one of Hollywood's top costume designers. She looked ready to step off the screen.

The only thing left to do now was to get married.

The trumpeters she had hired began to play and Corinne could feel the butterflies in her stomach begin to jump.

"Well," Grace announced with a sigh of resignation. "Let's get this damn show on the road."

IT WAS a day out of a dream.

The march down the aisle—perfect. The pitch of the trumpets—perfect. Her lines, rather her vows, were both written and spoken beautifully. Including the ones she had written for Matthew.

And when he kissed her for the first time as her husband, she allowed herself a few tears. After all, her makeup could be repaired in time for the pictures.

Corinne glowed with utter happiness. She knew it each time she looked into the mirror and she wanted to capture that glow for all time. She wanted her children and her grandchildren to look back and see exactly what true love was supposed to look like on a woman's face.

When they made it to the reception, she noted that the table settings were exactly as she had planned. The cake was a five-layer extravaganza covered with flowers that matched those she had in the church. The centerpieces were elegant. And the calligraphy on the place cards was faultless.

The band began to play and Corinne knew that soon she would be introduced as Mrs. Corinne Weatherby-Relic. She darted to the ladies' room for one last touch-up and then quickly reappeared on her husband's arm.

Matthew smiled down at her and gently touched his lips to hers. "Happy?"

"Ecstatic," she whispered to him.

"I heard your mother crying during the ceremony. She didn't sound so happy."

"No, she was just crying because she's so glad that I finally made the right decision," Corinne fibbed.

Matthew chuckled. It didn't matter what her family thought. Together, they were their own family now. Mr. Relic and Mrs. Weatherby-Relic. He supposed it sort of had a ring to it.

Corinne looked up at him and saw that he was glowing in much the same way she was. She thought again of how lucky she was to have finally woken up and seen him standing there right in front of her.

"Are you ready for our first dance?" he asked.

"Yes," she replied excitedly.

Someone called their names and they marched proudly into the reception area. There was laughter and applause, and Corinne saw that all eyes were on her.

It was an amazing moment.

It wasn't until Matthew let her step in front of him onto the dance floor that he realized that the back of her dress was caught up in her pink garter on her right leg.

Uh-oh, he thought, as he admired the flash of thigh she was giving him and the entire roomful of guests.

"Uh, Rinny..."

She twirled around back to him giving the group behind her the same peek-a-boo show he had just received. He heard their gasps and choked laughter and considered his options.

His first instinct was simply to inform her of the situation so she could fix the gown. But he'd made that promise to her about not revealing secrets publicly and he was betting that his promise also applied in this particular situation.

Acting quickly, he pulled her into his arms, grabbed a handful of the dress, and gave it a sharp tug, releasing it from the garter all within the confines of a coordinated dance move. His mother would have been proud.

The guests roared and applauded even louder this time.

"They're applauding our dancing," Corinne told him. "This time I can keep up with you. I took lessons."

"Okay," Matthew agreed, knowing it wasn't exactly the truth.

But it was okay because disaster had been avoided. The dress was around her ankles, the dance continued, and Corinne never knew what had happened.

Until she saw the video.

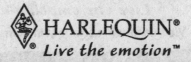

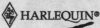

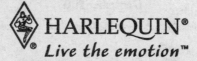

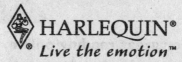